Amigas

Lights, Camera, Quince!

Amigas

Lights, Camera, Quince!

by Veronica Chambers

Created by Jane Startz
Inspired by Jennifer Lopez

Hyperion
New York

Copyright © 2010 Jane Startz Productions and Nuyorican Productions

All rights reserved. Published by Hyperion, an imprint of Disney Book Group. No part of this book may be reproduced or transmitted in any form or by any means, electronic or mechanical, including photocopying, recording, or by any information storage and retrieval system, without written permission from the publisher. For information address Hyperion, 114 Fifth Avenue, New York, New York 10011-5690.

Printed in the United States of America
First Edition
1 3 5 7 9 10 8 6 4 2

J689-1817-1-10152

Library of Congress Cataloging-in-Publication Data on file

ISBN 978-1-4231-2363-7

Designed by Jennifer Jackman

Visit www.hyperionteens.com

For Chris, Rose, Jeff, and Lily,
who do the father-daughter vals so well.
—V.C.

To my incredible husband, Peter Barton, and my great
children—and dear friends—Jesse, Kate, Zoë, and to all
my amigas, who make my life so rich and satisfying.
Many thanks to all and much love.
—J.S.

CHAPTER 1

"I'VE NEVER BEEN so exhausted in my entire life," Alicia Cruz groaned. "Exactly how many *quinceañeras* did we plan this summer?" she asked her friend and fellow Amigas Incorporated cohort Jamie Sosa.

"I'd say somewhere around . . . a gazillion," Jamie replied, her voice sounding strained as she stuffed a trash can with streamers.

Alicia nodded. The number felt right even though she knew Jamie had been exaggerating. She plopped down on the floor, not caring if it was filthy.

She was wearing her version of cleanup clothes: a white Ay! Vena Cava T, a pair of her dad's old cutoff shorts, and one of her mother's hand-me-down Gucci belts, for some retro bling. Even on a dedicated clean-up-and-run-errands day like this, Alicia believed that you had to bring it, fashionwise. Especially in Miami, where you never knew whom you were going to run into. But it was mid-August, not even lunchtime, and already over a hundred degrees. And as any native-born South Florida girl knows, heat rises. Sometimes, lying on the floor was the only option for staying cool, even if it didn't look fashionable.

Jamie quickly joined Alicia on the wooden planks of the gym floor. Ever the transplanted New Yorker, Jamie dressed like somebody out of a scene from the classic hip-hop movie *Beat Street*, and today she rocked a pair of vintage black Run-DMC frames. Her long brown hair was pulled to the side in a ponytail, and on her feet she wore a pair of limited-edition, only-available-in-Tokyo A Bathing Ape kicks.

"No one ever tells you about the ugly side of party planning," Jamie moaned, pointing to the piles and piles of garbage and recyclables they'd spent the whole morning picking up. The night before, they'd hosted a Hoops There It Is! *quinceañera*, complete with a free-throw contest and a dunking trampoline for the birthday girl who, though only in the tenth grade, was already six foot two and hoped to play in the WNBA. The party had been a lot of fun, but it had also been a ton of work. And because the school had been kind enough to let them host the event in the gym at no charge, they felt obligated to do a meticulous cleanup job.

"'Sup?" Carmen said, as she strolled into the gym and joined her friends on the floor. Carmen Ramirez-Ruben was the epitome of the girl who didn't try too hard. The fact that she was model-tall with flawless *caramelo* skin and bright hazel eyes didn't hurt, though. On a low-key day she could make even an understated wardrobe pop.

"What's up is, we've been working so hard all summer long," Jamie answered. "So, remind me: why aren't we filthy rich?"

"Because we're still learning," Alicia explained. "We would've made five thousand dollars this summer, remember. But we spent most of it on a new van for Gaz."

Gaspar Colón, Gaz for short, had resisted joining the girls and taking a spot on the floor. He'd recently been promoted to assistant manager at the Gap, where he worked part-time. To mark the occasion, he'd begun dressing nicer. Today he wore a new pair of pressed khakis, a plaid shirt, and a camel-colored tie. *Not* floor wear.

Now he looked down at Alicia and raised an eyebrow. "Hey, the Amigas crew didn't buy *me* anything," he protested, finally succumbing to the need to sit. Taking a towel from his gym bag, he joined the others on the floor. "The van is for *our* business. We need it for running errands, picking up flowers, catering. . . ."

"Shuttling disoriented *abuelas* from the wrong address . . ." Alicia said.

"To the right address," Gaz finished, reaching out and squeezing her hand.

Jamie rolled her eyes. "Are you guys still in the middle of that—what do you call it?"

"Flirtationship," Gaz and Alicia said at the same time.

"Is that even a real word?" Carmen asked.

"It's real to us," Gaz said, still holding on to Alicia's hand.

"And it means . . . ?" Carmen asked.

With Gaz holding her hand, Alicia felt the temperature in the room go up ten degrees. But she remained composed and simply replied, "It means we flirt. And we hold hands. But we don't go any further. . . ."

"Because our friendship is the most important thing," said Gaz, completing her sentence.

"Color me cynical," Jamie said. "But your 'flirtationship' sounds a lot like dating to me."

Alicia replied, "Our business, not your business."

"As opposed to the business of *quinceañeras*, which is *all* of our business," Carmen said. "Can you believe that a simple plan to help the new girl in town put together her *quince* has grown into such a huge business?"

"Well, *quinces* are major," Alicia pointed out.

"Especially in Miami," Jamie added.

The *quinceañera*, or Sweet Fifteen, was more than just a birthday party. In Latin families, the fifteenth year marked a major coming-of-age ritual: it was when a girl became a woman. Just three months before, Alicia had agreed to help a new girl, Sarita Lopez, plan her big day. This inspired Alicia to start Amigas Incorporated and rope her crew into helping. Along the way, Alicia, the de facto team leader, went a little *quince*-zilla, but in the end they'd all learned a lot about starting a business while keeping friendships intact. Luckily it had all turned out well, and now their in-boxes and voice mail were flooded with girls who wanted them to plan their *quinces*, too.

Alicia sat up and pulled her iPhone out of her purse. "Anyone up for a trip down memory lane?" Nodding, Gaz, Jamie, and Carmen gathered around her, eager for any excuse to postpone cleanup.

From the beginning, Alicia had been videotaping the parties they planned with her phone and putting the two-minute clips up on YouTube. They were Amigas Inc.'s best form of promotion—and *their* favorite form of entertainment.

Alicia now went to YouTube and called up a video of Sarita getting ready for her *quinceañera*. She was dressed in a Juicy Couture orange hoodie, a white tank, and navy blue shorts. Smiling at the camera she said, "Well, everybody, it's my big day. It's not even noon yet, but we've all been up for hours. My cousins and *tías* are in the living room, working on the favors."

The camera followed her into the small living room, where no fewer than thirty relatives sat on every available space. It looked like everyone was going into battle mode, not getting ready for a party.

Sarita was then seen going into her bedroom. "My *damas* are getting their hair and makeup done in here," she said.

In the sunny yellow bedroom, seven teenage girls in robes and slips crowded around the full-length mirror on the closet wall.

"There are seven *damas*, or girlfriends," Sarita explained. "There are seven *chambelanes*, who are usually your guy friends or your family. The *quince*—that's me—makes number fifteen!" She paused and gave the camera a huge grin. "Of course, I have to give a shout-out to Amigas Inc. for hooking the new girl up with the dopest *quince* in town!"

The clip ended, and Alicia scrolled through more videos until she found the one she wanted to view next. "Do you guys remember Ana Mary?"

"You mean, the Queen Bee?" Gaz asked, sarcastically.

On-screen, a girl stood in the ballroom of one of Miami's hip downtown hotels. Black and yellow streamers covered the wall, and barrels made to look like oversize honeycombs overflowed with sparkling apple cider.

"Those honeycombs were a nice touch," Carmen pointed out.

"Jamie's idea," Alicia said. "We should get you a T-shirt that says, *Innovator in the House*."

Jamie grinned. "As long as I get to design the logo."

Alicia nodded and hit PLAY on Ana Mary's clip.

"Hello, hello," Ana Mary said, flipping her long hair. "My colors are yellow and black, because my favorite animal is the bumblebee."

"She says it like a bumblebee is a type of pet," Jamie said, shaking her head.

"I've always liked bees, because I kind of see myself as the queen bee," Ana Mary went on, revealing a mouth full of braces. "Mess with me and you'll get stung."

"She's not lying about that," Carmen said.

"Tonight I'm wearing a custom-made dress inspired by Herve Leger," Ana Mary said, spinning around like a fashion model.

"'Custom-made,' meaning *I* remade that dress a

dozen times," Carmen growled. "First, she wanted it long, then she wanted it short. She wanted a train. She wanted a mini. She'd never even heard of Herve Leger before I showed her pictures of his dresses in *InStyle* magazine."

The group nodded, understanding their friend's frustration. Then they turned back to the phone's small screen.

"All of my *damas* are wearing exclusive Ana Mary designs," she continued, walking past a line of seven miserable-looking girls. "The *damas* are in yellow. My *chambelanes* are all in black."

Carmen reached over Alicia's shoulder and hit PAUSE. "She means, Exclusive Carmen Ramirez-Ruben designs. That girl . . . That girl . . ." She lunged toward the phone as if she could have strangled Ana Mary through it.

"We know, we know," Alicia said. "She was bad."

"She was more than bad, she was the *worst*," Carmen fumed.

"And that wasn't even the most irritating thing she did," Gaz said, taking the phone from Alicia, clearly enjoying the fact that Carmen, who was always the mellow one, was nearly ready to explode. "Let's roll the film and see just how bad she got."

He hit PLAY.

The clip showed Ana Mary turning away from a row of teenage boys, slumping against the ballroom wall, and smirking at the camera. "They all have crushes on me. They can't help it. I'm just so hot."

"*Ay,*" Carmen said. "Turn it off, she's giving me a headache!"

Headaches and self-absorbed girls aside, *quinceañeras* were important, and it was the group's job to make sure everyone was happy in the end—not an easy task, obviously.

With so much money on the table—some families had saved up for a girl's party from the moment she was born—and so much *familia* involved, things could get a little hairy. Moms went nuts over *quinces* and became mom-zillas. The *quince* could begin to throw attitude and turn into a *quince*-zilla.

Which is why Amigas Inc.'s cell phones had been ringing off the hook for the past few months. They were a one-stop *quince*-planning business—cool enough for girls to dig their style, and responsible enough to earn the trust of parents with big money at stake. They'd planned seven successful parties in three short months. And while the end result had been great, the cost was high. They were all seriously tired.

"We need a vacation," Alicia said after she'd put away her phone.

"That's the truth," Gaz answered.

Suddenly, Jamie sat bolt upright, all exhaustion gone. "Alicia! You're a genius!" Jamie exclaimed. "You guys should totally come with me to the Freestyle Convention in New York; it's going to be off the hook. My Facebook friend, Yoshi, is coming in from Osaka, and he said that I could show my sneaks at his booth. There's going to be hundreds of vendors—kicks men, 'boarders, clothing designers, DJs. Yoshi says that M.I.A. and Rye Rye are even going to do an unannounced concert."

Gaz's eyes lit up. "I could drop my band's CDs off at some record companies," he said. "There's this A&R guy I've been talking to on MySpace. I could look him up."

"It sounds amazing, and I would give anything to see the fabric shops in New York City," Carmen added, looking at Jamie. "But what about the little matter of school? Summer is almost over. You're my girl and everything, but my mom's a teacher; she won't go for me skipping classes."

"And while I may indeed be a 'genius,' you know Judge Cruz is tough on fun," Alicia added.

"No big deal," Jamie said, shrugging. "Freestyle is Columbus Day weekend. We leave Friday after school; we come back Monday night. No school missed."

"Do you know what I could do with three days in New York?" Alicia asked, her eyes widening at the possibility. "I could take a Limón dance class at the Ballet Hispanico. Of course, I'd have to check out Frida's *Self Portrait with Cropped Hair* at the Museum of Modern Art and Iliana Garcia's *Yo Quiero* at the Museo del Barrio. I'd need to go to dinner at Café Habana and lunch at 'wichcraft, because I love watching Tom Colicchio on *Top Chef*. I'd also have to go to Barney's to see the shoes, the Brooklyn Bridge for the views, and I would definitely swing by NYU Film School, because lately, I've been thinking that what I really want to do is direct."

When Alicia took a moment to breathe, Jamie, Gaz, and Carmen started laughing.

"What?" she said. "You're thinking I'm nuts if I don't see a Broadway show, right? I gotta do that, too."

"You're my girl," Jamie said, still chuckling, "but your definition of what *you* can do in three days and a normal person's definition of what *they* could do in three days are very, *very* different."

"*Exactamente,*" Gaz said.

"What he said," Carmen added.

"So, we go to New York for the weekend; Alicia goes for a week or a month," Gaz said, clearly warming up to the idea. "But *where* would we stay?"

It was a good question. The four friends lay back down on the floor. From overhead, they looked like the points of a star. Gaz's head and Alicia's touched slightly. Jamie was stretched out next to Alicia, and Carmen was squeezed between Jamie and Gaz. It was cool on the floor, and for a moment there was no sound except for the old-school air conditioners huffing and puffing.

"I've got mad cousins in New York," Jamie finally offered. "You could stay with my cousin Hector. Me and the girls could stay with my *tía* Digna and her kids."

"I hate to burst the bubble, but how are we going to raise enough money to go to New York?" Alicia asked.

"I've put every penny I've got into inventory for the show. If I sell all of my sneaks, I'll be rolling in loot," Jamie said.

"But that won't get us *to* New York. To cover all of our tickets and meals, we need to raise at least a thousand dollars," Gaz said matter-of-factly. "And that's *if* we get a sweet deal—and our parents say yes."

Alicia sat up, a determined look on her face. She never backed down from a challenge. "Well, you know what that means," she said. "We're just going to have to plan another *quince*."

Carmen, Jamie, and Gaz groaned, their eyes gazing at the piles of streamers, linen tablecloths, and empty soda cans that were piled up along the gym walls.

"I didn't even want to hear that word for at least another month," Gaz complained.

"It's the easiest, most fun way for us to raise enough money to go to New York," Alicia replied.

"I'm down," Jamie said at last, her eyes beginning to light up. "Raise enough money to go to Freestyle. Roll in there with my crew. It doesn't get any better than that. But there is another small problem. To make the money in time, we needed to have booked another *quince*, like, yesterday."

"I'll put a notice on our Web site," Alicia said. "There's bound to be some *chica* who waited until the very last minute to start planning the most important day of her life."

Jamie sat up. "Okay. But call me as soon as you get somebody."

"No need," Carmen said, stopping Jamie as she started to leave. "Amigas Incorporated can plan my *quince*. My birthday's October first."

CHAPTER 2

ALICIA AND CARMEN walked along the canals toward Carmen's house. This was one of Alicia's favorite parts of Miami. It was like a tropical version of her favorite children's book, *The Secret Garden*. There was a giant stone staircase that led into an amazingly green world. Palm trees created a canopy over the canals, and blue-green water trickled down, the tiniest of rivers. Some of the residents along the canal kept tiny wooden boats docked near their houses.

Alicia could always tell Carmen's house by the small turquoise-blue boat with the bright red number eight lying outside the front door. It was a model that one of Carmen's siblings had made—and then abandoned in short order. The 8 represented the eight people who lived in the house. Carmen's family was huge: there was her mother, Sophia; her stepdad, Christian; her older sister, Una; her brother, Tino; and her three stepsisters, Lindsay, Laura, and Lula.

At the moment, however, the idyllic setting was lost on Alicia. She had other things on her mind. "I can't believe I forgot your birthday," she groaned, putting her arm around her friend. "We've been so busy, but still . . . how could we forget the most important *quince* of the year?"

"Don't sweat it," Carmen said. "Really."

"I'm the worse best friend ever!" Alicia went on in an anguished voice.

"No, you're not." Carmen's eyes twinkled as she added, "I believe there's one other girl out there who forgot her best friend *and* her mom's birthday."

"I totally deserve that," Alicia sighed. "I'm hating myself right now. After you spent my birthday with me in Spain, I had every intention of making your day just as magical."

Carmen smiled. "It's not too late, *chica*. None of us expected Amigas Inc. to be such a big hit, and honestly, I've been struggling with what to do, exactly. One of the things I've loved about the *quinceañeras* that we've planned so far is that they really embody the spirit of each girl. They don't feel like all the ones we used to go to where you could tell that the moms were out of control and had decided on everything. . . ."

"Or the girls were spoiled brats."

"Exactly," said Carmen. "I mean, Sarita's astronaut theme was . . ."

"Off the hook," Alicia said. She loved it that she and Carmen could complete each other's sentences. It was as if they were in her favorite Frida Kahlo painting, where two girls were connected by one heart.

"Nilka's *'Top Chef'* party was too hot to handle. . . ."

"And too cold to hold," Alicia finished.

"The problem is, I still don't know what kind of *quinceañera* would be perfect for *me*," Carmen said as she opened the front door. Immediately, their ears were assaulted by noise. Alicia put her hands to her head jokingly. It was like when she grabbed her iPod out of her bag and didn't realize that the volume was turned way up until she put the headphones on—and the music exploded in her ears.

Carmen's older sister, Una, was making a smoothie in the kitchen and talking on the phone. Her brother, Tino, was watching a Mexican soccer game on the giant-screen TV in the living room. The twins, Laura and Lula, were playing Wii bowling in the dining room with three of their friends. Carmen's stepfather, Christian, meanwhile, sat at the dining table, miraculously listening to classical music and reading Shakespeare, as if he were ensconced in the peace and quiet of the British Museum.

"Well, hello, Carmen," Christian said, standing up. He was from England and the blond, blue-eyed, polar opposite of Carmen's dark-haired, chocolate-eyed mom.

"And, Alicia," he added, giving her air-kisses on each cheek. "You haven't been around in ages."

"Actually, I come over every day. But there's always so many people here you never notice," Alicia said playfully. She had just the tiniest, crumb-size, speck of a crush on Carmen's stepdad, which she could never tell Carmen about, because, well, that would just be too weird. She blamed it on the accent.

Christian laughed. "Well done, Alicia."

"Where's Lindsay?" Carmen asked, glancing toward the other younger kids. Lindsay was eight years old and Carmen's mini-me, following her everywhere.

"Band camp," Christian answered. "Those tubas don't play themselves."

Carmen nodded, and then she and Alicia went into the kitchen, where Una deigned to nod at them. This was a step up from the usual treatment. And frankly, more than they expected. Una was about to be a senior at Coral Gables High. A very popular senior. Throughout their freshman year, she had refused to speak to them at all in public places. She was captain of the dance team, a star member of the drama club, and secretary of state for the Regional Southeast Conference of the Model UN. Which basically meant she was a diva, but a smart diva. Deep down, Alicia really admired Una, but that was another thing she could never really tell her friend. Maybe this year Una would be nicer. Maybe.

Ignoring her sister, Carmen tossed Alicia a plastic fork and a roll of paper towels. Then she took a container of cut mangoes from the fridge. She opened it and sprinkled black pepper on the mango slices, grabbed a fork, and said, "Let's talk outside. I can't even hear myself think in here."

Once away from the noise, Carmen made a beeline for the wooden rowboat that was docked in the canal behind her house. She climbed in, and Alicia followed. They used to sit in the boat and talk all the time when they were little, but they hadn't done that in ages. Alicia didn't realize how much she had missed it until now.

For a moment they were silent as they enjoyed their snack and the quiet.

"If I ever get stuck on an island, like on *Lost*, I'd be happy as long as I had peppered mango," Alicia said, licking her lips. "Peppered mango and Gaz."

"Me, too," Carmen said.

Alicia smiled mischievously. "Oh, really?"

Carmen giggled. "You know what I meant. Mangoes are all I need. Gaz is one hundred percent yours sweetie. Now, can we focus? What are we going to do about my *quince*? We need a theme—and fast."

"Agreed. There can be no corners cut on this one. I've heard Carmen Ramirez-Ruben is a very demanding customer," Alicia said, her eyes twinkling.

"Probably our toughest one yet," Carmen said, playing along.

"She's going to hate your dress design," Alicia said, shaking her head.

Carmen nodded. "*At least* the first ten sketches."

"She's going to be demanding," Alicia insisted.

"But not *too* bad," Carmen said in defense of herself.

"You're right. She just knows what she wants," Alicia agreed.

"That's the thing, Lici," Carmen said, finally dropping the use of the third person. "I don't know what I want. Not really. And I've got a lot riding on this *quince*. A lot of family expectations." Her expression grew somber.

"Hey," Alicia said. "Don't get down. We'll work this all out. How about we take this boat for a ride? Doesn't your mom always say that you think better out on the water?"

Carmen nodded. "She's got a point."

The two girls pushed the little rowboat into the canal, and Carmen expertly took the oars. As her friend's long arms moved the oars through the water, Alicia waited patiently. She knew Carmen needed to be left with her thoughts for a moment. But soon, she felt she couldn't take it anymore. She'd had a burst of inspiration.

"Coming up with a theme for your *quince* is the easiest thing I've done all year!" she cried, breaking into her friend's silent contemplation. "You've wanted to be a designer since you were old enough to say, *platform heel*. What do you say to a *Project Runway*–themed *quince*? It could be *wunderbar*."

Carmen giggled, even though Alicia's imitation of Heidi Klum left a lot to be desired.

"I know that's what you'd expect," Carmen said, "but it's not exactly what I want. I certainly love fashion, but I love my family even more."

"*Dime,*" Alicia said, taking in the multicolored houses that lined the canal. "So, then, what kind of event *does* my best friend want?"

"Well, you remember my *Abuela* Ruben? My dad's

mother?" Carmen asked. It was a rhetorical question. All of Carmen's friends knew her Jewish Argentinean grandmother. She only came from Buenos Aires to visit once a year, but she cut quite a wide swath when she did. *Abuela* Ruben was the only woman in South Florida whom any of them had ever met who could make both salsa *and* fierce potato latkes. "She really wanted me to have a bat mitzvah," Carmen went on.

"But that argument was done and over way back in junior high," Alicia pointed out. "Wasn't it?"

Carmen rolled her eyes. "It started on my twelfth birthday, when a nice Jewish girl like me *should* have been planning her bat mitzvah and hasn't stopped. . . ."

"Half Jewish," Alicia corrected her.

Carmen began to paddle the boat with increasing speed. "*Abuela* Ruben says there's no such thing as half. She wants to know if I'm ready to be punished in the next life for the sins I've committed in this one."

Alicia let out a long whistle. "Your *abuela* really knows how to lay a guilt trip."

"Are you asking me or telling me?" Carmen said playfully. "The thing is, even though my mom and my stepdad raised me in the Catholic church, I do feel Jewish. I'd love to have a *quince* that honors my culture and doesn't ignore my religion."

Alicia knitted her eyebrows as she tried to think of the perfect solution. Coming up with on-the-spot themes was quickly becoming one of her specialties. But a Jewish Latina *quinceañera* was going to require a lot more research and a lot more thought than any themes she'd dreamed up before.

"I'm going to have to let this idea cook a little," Alicia finally said. "Can I get back to you tomorrow?"

"Sure," Carmen said, turning the boat around and rowing back toward home. "I didn't expect miracles."

"But you deserve one," Alicia said. Then she asked, "Do you think your *abuela* Ruben will even come to your *quince*? What about the church ceremony?"

"I don't know, *chica*," Carmen said as she and Alicia took off their shoes and stood knee-deep in the canal, preparing to pull the boat in, "but she's my *abuela*, and I love her. I know she's disappointed, but I'd love for my *quinceañera* to change her mind. Show her what my faith means, even if it is not in the traditional, Jewish sense."

"But will that make *you* happy?" Alicia asked, pushing her sunglasses up on her head so that she could look her friend in the eye.

"I think it will," Carmen replied, sounding far from convinced.

Looking at her friend's forlorn expression, it became

suddenly very clear to Alicia: this had to be the most special Amigas Incorporated party yet. Grouchy *abuelas* or not.

Later that night, after dinner and when they were alone, Carmen double-checked with her mom about hiring Amigas Inc. Christian had taken the rest of the family to the mall. The youngest girls wanted ice cream, Tino needed soccer cleats, and Una went along because, well, she never missed an opportunity to shop.

At fourteen, Carmen was already several inches taller than her mother. When they stood next to each other, you could see that she had the same thin frame as her mother, plus the same heart-shaped face and café au lait–colored skin. But Carmen always looked as though she were wearing six-inch stilettos, even when she was standing in her bare feet. And at five feet two inches tall, Carmen's mom, Sophia, who was head of the math department at C. G. High, often got mistaken for one of her students when she dashed through the hall, her long ponytail swinging behind her.

"The fact that Amigas is planning your *quince* means less work for me," Sophia said when Carmen finally brought it up. As they talked, she opened the dishwasher so Carmen could stack while she rinsed.

Moments like this, when it was just she and her mother, were Carmen's favorites, even if they were spent doing something as mundane as washing the dishes.

"Listen to that!" she said to her mother.

"I don't hear anything," Sophia said, turning off the water.

"*Exactly,*" Carmen said, and both she and her mother laughed. Sophia started rinsing the glasses and Carmen placed them carefully on the top rack of the dishwasher.

"You and your friends have done such a wonderful job planning the other *quinceañeras* I know you'll do a great job," Sophia went on, getting back to the topic at hand. "I also know you'll mind the budget, which is not very big. But I have to say, I've been wondering why you haven't started planning sooner. I've been asking you what you want to do for months now. Your birthday is less than six weeks away. You know, more than most, just how much work it is to plan a *quinceañera.*"

"I know, *Mamita*," Carmen said, taking the dark blue and orange clay heirloom plates from her mother and putting them into the machine gently. She paused, then added, "I've been really struggling, because I know no matter how great a *quince* we have, it's never going to be good enough for *Abuela* Ruben."

Carmen's mother turned off the water and wiped her wet hands on her jeans. Then she put her arms around her daughter. "*Querida*, it's *your* day. Which means, the only person you have to please is you."

Carmen could feel her eyes welling up with tears. Her mom made it sound so easy. She let her head rest on her mother's shoulders and wished, for a moment, that she was a little kid again so she could crawl into her mom's lap and not have to make any decisions.

"It's just that I want *Abuela* Ruben to be proud of me," Carmen said, her voice choked with tears.

"She is—and she will be. She wouldn't come all the way from Buenos Aires for your birthday if she didn't know how special your *quinceañera* was."

"She would've liked it more if I'd had a bat mitzvah," Carmen pointed out sadly.

Her mother, ever the cheerleader, held up a hand. "Stop projecting, *niña*. You can't have any idea what your grandmother is thinking."

"Oh, yeah, I do," Carmen said. "It's not like she hides it. Case in point: the last time she called, she said, 'I would've liked it much better if you had had a bat mitzvah, like a nice Jewish girl.'"

Carmen's mother smiled and tried to think of a way to put a positive spin on this startlingly clear piece of information. "Well . . . I mean . . ." Then she just shook her head. "I don't know what to say."

Carmen laughed. "My sentiments exactly."

Her mother took a seat on the high-backed kitchen chair. "Come," she said, "sit on my lap."

Carmen raised an eyebrow. "Yeah, right. I'll break you *and* the chair."

Her mom shook her head. "I'm stronger than I look. *Venga*, just for a minute."

Carmen walked over and sat, tentatively, on her mother's lap, her long legs stretched out to the side.

As her mother combed through her daughter's hair with her fingers, the way she had used to right before she dropped her off for school when Carmen was a little girl, Carmen felt some of the pressure ease. Maybe things would all be okay. Maybe she was just overreacting.

"It'll work out," her mother said after a few minutes, echoing Carmen's thoughts.

"I know it will, *Mamita*," she said, kissing her mother on the cheek.

She had to hope they were both right.

CHAPTER 3

THE NEXT afternoon, the *amigas*—and Gaz—met up in South Beach for a planning meeting. Alicia's dad had offered to give her and Carmen a ride on his way to a tennis game, so they were the first to arrive. At night, Bongos Café was a strictly over-twenty-one hot spot. But during the day, the café served lunch and the friends loved to hang out in the back room, where the banging beats, Andy Warhol portraits of Gloria Estefan, and virgin *mojitos* had a cool vibe that was a cut above the usual Cuban fare.

Bongos also happened to be the perfect spot for celebrity sightings. This day did not disappoint. As soon as the girls walked in, they noticed Sharon Kim and the Channel 6 news crew setting up in a corner of the restaurant.

Sharon anchored the local eleven o'clock news, but she was best known for her Sunday morning talk show,

¡Hoy en Miami!, where she always snagged interviews with the hottest stars in town. Everything about her high-wattage personality made it clear that she hoped to do much more than be the star of a local news or gossip program. At the moment, she was wearing a tomato red designer dress that Alicia was willing to bet good money was a Michael Kors, because she'd seen it in the look book her mother's salesperson had sent from Saks. The flashes of red sole from the bottoms of her black stilettos revealed that Sharon's shoes were Christian Louboutins. And Alicia was pretty confident that the diamond studs in her ears weren't fake. As she looked around the room, Sharon's grin was as wide as the I-95 freeway (post the expansion construction).

"I wonder who she's interviewing today," Carmen whispered, in awe at seeing their favorite news reporter live and in person.

"It's Miranda Cosgrove, but she's not here yet," said a supercute waiter as he walked by carrying a giant platter of rice and beans. "But you didn't hear it from me."

He winked at Carmen and continued past her.

Alicia and Carmen turned to each other and whispered, "Omigod—," then bit their fists.

The hostess, a pretty Blake Lively look-alike, finally

took notice of them. "Your table is ready, *girls*," she said, making both Carmen and Alicia roll their eyes.

The minute they got settled at their table, Carmen whipped out an imaginary microphone and did her best Sharon Kim impersonation. "Miss Cruz! You look simply stunning. What *are* you wearing today?" This was a game she and Alicia had been playing since they were in middle school. They called it "Red Carpet Arrivals."

Alicia tossed her hair, and said, in a fake British accent, "Well, Carmen, today I'm wearing a black Proenza Schouler leather halter, a white miniskirt from the Gap, and a pair of hand-me-down Louboutin espadrilles from my mom."

"You're simply flawless," Carmen said, emulating the accent.

"And what are *you* wearing today, Miss Ramirez-Ruben?" Alicia said, taking a turn at holding the pretend microphone.

Before Carmen could answer, they heard someone clear his throat.

"I hate to interrupt what is clearly an important media moment, but do you have time for me to take your order?" the waiter asked, a smile tugging at the corners of his mouth. It was the same cute waiter who had passed by and spoken to them earlier.

The two girls stifled a serious case of the giggles. Just how long had he been standing there? Without a doubt he was a MWAH of the highest order (MWAH meaning, Man, What a Hottie!). His hair was buzzed short, he had bright, friendly eyes, and a long, lean build.

Alicia quickly recovered. "We're waiting for two more friends. But we know what they want. We'll take an order of *papas rellenas*. . . ."

"Yum," said Carmen.

"Fried green plantains with garlic sauce," Alicia continued.

"Yum," added Carmen.

"Two stuffed green plantain cups. One with shrimp creole, one with *ropa vieja*."

The waiter turned to Carmen and smiled. "No yum with that?"

She blushed. "Nope, just two virgin *mojitos*, please."

At that moment, Gaz appeared; he slid into the table across from the girls and said, "And one real *mojito*."

The waiter, whose name tag read DOMINGO, looked at Gaz suspiciously. "Hey, man, do you have ID?"

Gaz looked embarrassed. "Um, I forgot it at home."

"Well, I'm seventeen, and I'm pretty sure that

you're not older than me," Domingo said. "So that'll be three virgin *mojitos*. Besides, we don't serve alcohol at lunchtime."

With that, he walked away.

Alicia gave Gaz a mock stern look. "What's up with that? Did you really just try to order alcohol?"

Gaz shrugged. "I dunno. You were flirting with him. I just wanted to seem older."

Alicia smiled, balled up a napkin, and threw it at Gaz's forehead. "I was not flirting with him. Carmen was. The only person I have a flirtationship with is you."

"Good," Gaz said, reaching for her hand.

"Just a reminder," Carmen pointed out. "*Flirtationship*—not a real word, not a real thing."

Alicia smiled. "It's real to us."

"I love you, *chica*, but I've also known you for a long time. I remember when Santa Claus and the tooth fairy were real to you, too," Carmen teased.

A short while later, Domingo returned with their food, and reluctantly, Alicia and Gaz stopped holding hands and began to eat.

Jamie finally arrived and slid into the booth next to Gaz. "Wassup, *chicas*?"

"*Chicos*," Gaz practically growled. "In Spanish, when you're referring to both men and women, you say *chicos*."

Jamie shrugged. "You know my Spanish isn't that good. But whatever; *so* not the point. Much bigger issues at hand." She took a flyer out of her messenger bag. "Check this out. We've got some competition. Simone Baldonado started a Sweet Sixteen–planning business."

All three of them groaned.

Simone Baldonado was the richest girl at school and, as far as the friends were concerned, the most obnoxious. Her *quinceañera*, with its Princesses Through the Ages theme, had been the perfect encapsulation of Simone—OTT, or "over the top." It wasn't a surprise she was a bit of a brat. Her parents owned the Coronado hotel, *the* South Beach hot spot for the rich, famous, and fabulous. They lived in a massive penthouse suite on the top floor and had amazing views.

Alicia could hardly believe that once upon a time, for about eight months in the second grade, she and Simone had been friends. More than that, they had been *mejores amigas*, the *best* of friends. Alicia tried not to think about it too much. Who could explain the choices a person made when she was seven years old? She didn't even remember entirely when Simone had started hating her guts. But she did remember that, ever since that mysterious moment, Simone had always had something catty to say and was always, *always*, trying to mess with Alicia—and now Amigas Incorporated.

Alicia looked down at Simone's flyer and shrugged. "*A*, this picture of Simone makes her look demented. *B*, who cares about Sweet Sixteens? We do *quinceañeras*."

Jamie pointed to the line underneath the main one. The one that read, WE DO QUINCES, TOO.

As if she'd been waiting and watching for them to find her flyer, Simone suddenly appeared in the restaurant. She walked over to their table, trailed by her best friend, Ellen Thomas.

"What are you doing here?" Alicia asked.

"Having lunch; it's a free country, you know," Ellen replied, speaking for Simone.

Wherever Simone was, Ellen usually wasn't far behind. The two girls were like Frick and Frack. Alicia wasn't surprised to see that today the two girls were wearing matching pink plaid Burberry polos with pink shorts and pale pink Tretorn sneakers.

"Congratulations, Ellen," Alicia said, sweetly.

"For what?" Ellen asked, looking ever so pleased with herself.

"You win first prize for not having a single original thought of your own," Alicia answered.

"Sticks and stones," Simone purred sarcastically. "I see you've gotten wind of our incredibly viral marketing campaign."

Gaz held up the piece of paper. "You mean the flyer? I thought *viral* meant 'online.'"

"Viral, grassroots, whatever," Simone scoffed. "I've already gotten twelve calls, and these just went up yesterday afternoon."

The four friends tried not to gulp obviously. Twelve calls in one day? They'd been in business for months and were happy if they got twelve calls a *week*.

"It's because your mom is offering a thirty percent discount on dresses from her boutique," Alicia said, pointing to one of the bullet points on the flyer. "Nobody else can compete with that."

"So what? It's a *business*. A discount is a marketing tool used by *businesses*. Not amateurs like you guys," Simone said. "My family has owned the top hotel in South Beach for three generations. My mother's boutique is the number-one seller of party dresses. I am *way* more entitled to plan *quinceañeras* than you are."

"Except for the fact that you didn't have the idea, you thief," Alicia fumed. "You stole it from us."

"Don't hate the player, hate the game, *chicas*!" Simone flashed a huge grin, then turned on her heel, giving the group a little wave. She had accomplished what she had come to do.

Gaz groaned and called out, "*Chico*. As in, masculine. As in, sitting right here."

But Simone and Ellen were being seated at a table on the patio and didn't even pretend to hear.

Jamie patted his shoulder. "Poor baby. Don't worry, we all know you're a guy. . . ."

"That's why we keep you around," Alicia said, winking at Gaz from across the table. "To carry all the heavy stuff."

She turned her attention back to Simone's flyer. Even if she couldn't admit it aloud, the flyer was irksome to her. "This is not a problem," she said confidently. "Miami is the *quince* capital of America. There's plenty of work to go around. No way is Simone going to steal our shine. Let's get back to planning Carmen's party. That's what matters."

"Agreed," Gaz said. Then he added, "So how *do* we do a cool Jewish Latina *quince*?"

"Well, your *abuela* is bummed that you didn't have a bat mitzvah, right?" Jamie asked Carmen as she picked at the scraps of fried plantains remaining on the serving plate.

"Right," Carmen said, nodding.

"So, maybe we make it a mash-up, a *quince*-mitzvah!"

Carmen guffawed, and the *mojito* she was drinking nearly came out of her nose.

"You are one classy lady," Alicia said, grinning.

At that moment, Domingo came by with another tray of *mojitos*. "I thought it looked like you all might want some refills," he said, putting down four ice-cold glasses garnished with fresh mint.

"We might want refills. Yes," said Jamie, saucily. "But do we want to *pay* for refills? No."

"Then they are on me," he said, turning to Carmen and winking.

Once Domingo was out of earshot, Alicia bumped shoulders with Carmen. "He totally likes you," she said.

"Totes," Jamie agreed.

"You think?" Carmen said. "Is he too old for me?"

"Who cares?" Jamie retorted. "He would be the hottest *chambelán* this town has ever seen."

Gaz groaned. "Tell me why I'm not chilling with my guy friends right now."

"Because you don't have any," Alicia replied, playfully.

"Come on, what about Hector?" Gaz said. Hector was a DJ that Carmen had gone out with once. "He's my boy. It's just that he's spinning at some car show today."

The restaurant had been packed when they arrived, but now all of their food was gone. As were most of the people. Dropping the topic of Gaz's friends—or lack thereof—Carmen tapped her watch. "My mom is coming to pick me up in twenty minutes. Ideas, people. I need ideas."

"So, *quince*-mitzvah is not going to work?" Jamie asked earnestly.

Carmen shook her head. "I don't think so, *niña*."

"A mash-up is a good idea," Gaz said, "but maybe not so literal."

"How about 'Fifteen Is the New Thirteen'?" Jamie said. "We could do a whole Jewish *Wizard of Oz*: you're Dorothy, and you've got to find your way back to Israel."

"No!" Carmen said, bursting into laughter. "Please, please stop. Besides I don't think anyone in my family has even been to Israel."

Alicia raised an eyebrow. "Maybe we could get everyone to wear those cool red string Kabbalah bracelets, like Madonna."

Carmen laughed even harder. "I don't think *Abuela* Ruben even knows who Madonna is, and if she does, I'm sure that she doesn't think she's a nice Jewish girl."

"Let's go back to the bat mitzvah idea," Jamie suggested. "I know it's a rite of passage like the *quinceañera* is, except many Jewish girls have theirs starting at twelve and Latin girls have theirs at fifteen."

"You should've split the difference and had yours at fourteen, Lati-jew-na style," Gaz said.

Carmen and Alicia laughed.

"Lati-jew-na—is that even a word?" Jamie asked.

"It is now," Gaz said proudly.

"Sorry, *chico*. No, it isn't," Carmen said.

"What does the word *bat mitzvah* actually mean?" Jamie asked, pressing on. She took out her sketch pad and a black Sharpie and drew the word in cool graffiti script. She held up the pad. "How dope would that look on a pair of high-top Converse sneakers?"

Everyone nodded. Pretty dope, they seemed to agree.

"*Bat mitzvah* means Daughter of the Commandments," Carmen explained.

Alicia bounced up and down in her seat. "That's it! The theme is Daughter of the Commandments."

"Catchy," Jamie said, sarcastically.

"Sounds like a super good time," Gaz added.

"Well, the first commandment is, *Thou shalt not interrupt*," Alicia said. "We get a guy to dress like Moses— maybe even Carmen's dad. You know he's a clown. And instead of breaking the tablets, he breaks a giant matzo piñata."

Carmen, Jamie, and Gaz were silent.

"Genius, huh?" Alicia asked.

Her friends exchanged looks.

"You ragged on me for *quince*-mitzvah," Jamie finally said, incredulous.

"You made fun of Lati-jew-na," Gaz added, solemnly, shaking his head.

At last, Carmen patted her best friend on the shoulder. "You're done, kid; that idea really, *really* sucked." Then, looking at her watch again, she added, "Okay, meeting over. On account of the fact that the pressure is getting to Lici, and she's losing her mind. And my mom is coming. Let's reconvene—when we aren't so fried."

CHAPTER 4

THE NEXT DAY, Carmen went to visit her father, Javier Ruben, on the set of his latest project. He produced *telenovelas*, which were Spanish soap operas. Except, instead of going on and on for years like the soap operas in the U.S., *telenovelas* were usually on five days a week, but for only six months.

Javier Ruben was quite a successful producer, although he was constantly complaining that television audiences in Argentina, where his series aired, were nowhere near as loyal as the viewers in Mexico and Colombia.

"If I were *colombiano*," he was always saying, "I'd be a rich man. I'd have a condo in Buenos Aires and a house on Fishers Island, next to Oprah."

As it was, he did quite well. His condo on Biscayne Bay had panoramic views of the city. But that was just how Javier Ruben was, ambitious—and just a little bit competitive. The phrase grass is always greener applied to him—110 percent.

Carmen's Spanish wasn't good enough to translate the torrent of Spanish her father was barking into his cell phone when she arrived at his office on the set, but she understood enough to get that he wasn't exactly happy with the distribution deal for his latest project. He held up one finger, indicating that she should wait, then pointed at the phone and made a gesture implying that the person on the other end of the line was nuts.

When he hung up a few minutes later, he sprang out of his director's chair and kissed Carmen on both cheeks.

It was from her father that Carmen had inherited her height. But she wasn't as tall as he was; she still had to look up to see into his eyes. He was basketball-player tall. And basketball-player handsome.

Today, he was dressed in a perfectly pressed white linen shirt, khakis, and a pair of Gucci loafers. There was no mistaking him for one of the associate producers or camera technicians running around the set. He looked too professional.

"This is only day three of shooting, so things are a little bananas," her dad explained, hooking his arm around Carmen's. "Let's walk. My office is too stuffy."

The crew had set up in the lobby of one of Miami's old art deco hotels, and there were at least a hundred people dashing back and forth between the corner of the room where the actors were rehearsing their lines under the hot lights, and the other parts of the ballroom where stations had been set up for catering, hair and makeup, and wardrobe.

"So, what's this one called?" Carmen asked. She loved the energy of film and television production. She'd been visiting sets since she was a little girl, but nevertheless her eyes widened as she took in the flawless makeup of one of the actresses, the flirtatious smile of the man running through his lines with an associate producer, and all the other people, behind the scenes, who made it happen.

"*Dolores La Doble,*" Javier said.

"And what's it about?" Carmen asked.

"What are they ever about? *El drama que es la vida,* the drama that is life." Javier gestured to the handsome actor in the makeup chair. "He's a soccer referee living a humdrum life in the suburbs outside of Buenos Aires. Then he inherits a fortune from the wealthy *tía* he never knew he had. He meets Dolores, a beautiful woman who turns out to be a gold digger, or so his duplicitous brother would have him believe. So he throws Dolores out on her ear, but can't stop thinking about her. He goes on a hiking trip in the mountains and in a simple village meets a girl who reminds him so much of Dolores. What's the connection between the two women? Are they merely doppelgängers, two people who look remarkably alike but aren't related? Or are more sinister forces at work? Tune in next week and every week for the next six months, to find out."

Carmen rubbed her hands together. "I like it. It's juicy."

"Juicy is my business," her father said.

Carmen did not need to ask who was playing the role of Dolores, because for the past five years, almost all of her father's *telenovelas* had starred his wife, Natalia. Blond, blue-eyed, and unapologetically glamorous, Natalia had never pretended to be interested in being a stepmother to Carmen and her siblings. She treated them like honored family friends, which wasn't nearly as bad as it sounded or as bad as some other stepparents sounded.

As if on cue, Natalia entered the ballroom, dressed in a long red designer gown with ruby nails and lips to match. Her entourage followed close behind.

"*Hola, chica,*" she said, greeting Carmen with a kiss on each cheek. "*Qué hay?*"

"Not much," Carmen said. "This new show sounds great."

"It's most fabulous; I'm playing two roles—a blond and a brunette," Natalia said. Her accent was slight and sexy. "Speaking of which, I have to go now for fittings for my country character. Ciao-ciao."

She kissed Javier on the cheek and then strode away, followed by a small phalanx of assistants, costumers, makeup artists, agents, and script supervisors. Carmen could smell her Carolina Herrera perfume for several minutes after she left.

Her sister Una was always complaining about Natalia, but Carmen had no problem with her "step-mom." Before Natalia, Javier had dated a string of MAWs—model/actress/whatevers. Most of them had been just a few years older than Una and Carmen; none of them had had any real talent or potential for success. Carmen had just begun to worry that her dad was turning into *that guy* when he met Natalia. She was a former pop star turned actress and was at least born in the same decade as Javier. Moreover, she seemed to make him very happy. To Carmen, that counted for a lot.

If only she could figure out a way to make *Abuela* Ruben happy. . . .

"Can we talk somewhere, Dad?" Carmen asked. "This actually isn't a social call."

"Of course," Javier said. "Let's walk out to the pool. We can talk there."

Carmen followed her father out to one of the three pools at the hotel. He motioned for a waiter as they sat down, and a young man with dark hair showed up seconds later.

"I'd love a large Pellegrino," Javier said.

"Two glasses," Carmen added.

"And lemon," they both said, in unison.

"So, what's going on, *muñeca brava*?" Javier asked.

"Well, you know my *quinceañera* is coming up," Carmen said.

Javier nodded. "Of course. I want to chip in. I'll send your mother a check."

Carmen shook her head. She loved her father, but every once in a while, she thought, it would have been great if the man who managed a crew of over a hundred people and could name every item on his multimillion dollar film budget could think of something besides a check to try to make her happy.

"*Quince*, huh?" Javier went on, unaware of her musings. "That's a big one. Do you want a car?"

Carmen raised her eyebrow. "Can you afford three

cars? Because you know Tino and Una would each want one, too. Plus, I'm only turning fifteen—not sixteen."

Javier sighed. "Well, when you put it that way, maybe that's not such a great idea."

"Dad," Carmen said, "this isn't about a gift. I need your advice."

The waiter returned with their bottled water. Carmen poured herself a glass and took a sip.

"I didn't have a bat mitzvah, and *Abuela* Ruben has been mad at me for two years," she said in a rush.

"Two years? That's nothing," Javier said. "Do you know how long she held a grudge against me?"

"Dad, not about you," Carmen reminded him.

"You're right, you're right," Javier said. "Continue."

"She's coming for my *quinceañera*," Carmen said.

"Wait, *Abuela* Ruben is coming to Miami?" Javier asked. "When?"

"Six weeks, Dad," Carmen said, trying to keep the impatience out of her voice.

"Great, I'll make sure Natalia is out of town."

Ignoring her father's selfish comment, she went on. "I want to bring some kind of religious element into my *quinceañera* so *Abuela* knows that I value the part of me that's half Jewish."

"Sounds good, *niña*," Javier said, seeming distracted.

"But that's the thing, I don't really know a lot about my Jewish heritage."

Both father and daughter stared straight ahead, taking in the vista of the infinity pool and the way it seemed to spill into the ocean. It was true, it was hard for Javier to focus, and he was perfectly content to leave the majority of the parenting of his children to Carmen's mother and stepfather. He and Natalia lived a different life. At the same time, he loved his daughter, and he could see that she was struggling with her current dilemma.

"I think you're making a big mistake in thinking that you're half Jewish and half Latina," Javier said finally. "In Buenos Aires, my family is *all* Jewish and *all* Latin. It's not like an Oreo cookie. You can't separate the different parts."

Carmen gave her father a weak smile. "Wow, Dad. That was actually kind of deep."

Javier held a hand to his heart. "Are you teasing me?"

"No," Carmen said. "Totally serious."

Javier puffed out his chest a bit and continued. "Don't think about Judaism as a formal institution. To tell you the honest truth, I don't think I've been in a synagogue since Natalia and I got married. But I think about being Jewish every day. Think about what it means to you personally; that's the only way to honor your heritage in any kind of a meaningful way."

Before he could say more, a young female production assistant wearing a baseball cap, a T-shirt that said REALITY SHOW RUNNER-UP, and a walkie-talkie on a belt buckle approached them. "Excuse me, Mr. Ruben," she said meekly. "They're ready for you on set."

Javier stood up and kissed his daughter on the cheek. "*Querida*, I've got to go."

"Go, go," Carmen said. "Thanks for the advice. I really appreciate it."

"You will get back to me about what you want for a *quinceañera* present?" he asked.

"Not a car?" Carmen called out, playfully.

"Not a car!" her father said over his shoulder as he followed the production assistant back to the set.

For a moment, Carmen stood there, just enjoying the feeling of a good heart-to-heart. Then a voice startled her.

"Excuse me," a tall young woman nearby interjected. "I hate to be rude, but I couldn't help but overhear. Did you say, '*quinceañera*'?" She came closer.

"Yeah?" Carmen said, surprised.

"Are you about to have one?" the young woman asked.

Carmen nodded.

The woman handed her a card and said, "My name's Mary Kenoyer, and I'm a producer for *¡Hoy en Miami!* with Sharon Kim."

Carmen beamed. "My friends and I love Sharon Kim!"

Mary nodded as if this were nothing new. "Yeah, she's pretty awesome. Listen, we're planning a competition to see who can throw the most spectacular *quinceañera.*"

Carmen raised an eyebrow. "Well, in that case, let me give you *my* card. We're planning my party as we speak."

Mary looked down and read it aloud: *"Amigas Incorporated,* Quinceañera *Planners."* She glanced up. "It seems this is my lucky day. That's killing two birds with one stone. When is your event?"

"Early October," Carmen said.

"Perfect. Well, talk it over with your parents and the rest of your team, and call me so we can try and work something out," Mary said. "The station gives each team a budget of a thousand dollars to work with. There's lots of fun prizes, and it's pretty cool being on TV, but being filmed for a competition can get really intense. We'd be following you all the time. You'd have to make sure you're all up for it."

"Um, okay," Carmen said, trying to stay cool. Mary waved good-bye and Carmen made her way through the hotel lobby and outside.

Then she lost her cool. Squealing, she called Alicia. "You'll never believe who I just met!" Carmen cried.

CHAPTER 5

LATER THAT afternoon, the three girls met at Alicia's house to discuss the television project. Gaz was at work but had put in his two cents via e-mail.

The Cruz family had done well for themselves—Alicia's mother was a judge and her dad was deputy mayor—and lived in one of the most chichi parts of Coral Gables. Jamie and Carmen practically lived at Alicia's house, which was why on that day they didn't think anything of following her down the long hallway and changing into their bathing suits in her bedroom.

Living in the Miami area meant that all three girls owned many, many swimsuits, and their favorite thing to do was to swap, mix, and match their tops and bottoms. Carmen wore a hot pink bikini top with a pair of leopard-print boy shorts. Alicia slipped into the leopard-print top and a pair of black bikini bottoms. Jamie rifled through her friend's bags until she came up with a pale pink check Burberry bikini top.

"What do you think of this with my khaki board shorts?" Jamie asked, trying the two pieces together.

"Perfecto," said Alicia.

"Do you think we're nuts putting all this effort into styling and profiling when we're just hanging out at your house and nobody will see us?" Carmen asked as the three girls walked back toward the kitchen.

"Hey, I'm not nobody," Maribelle Puentes said, reaching to pull Alicia into a big bear hug. The polite Latino way of greeting a friend was with a kiss on the cheek—one if you were in a rush, two if you had more time and were being European and chic. But Maribelle didn't play that. She was a hugger, through and through. After squeezing Alicia tightly, she greeted Jamie and Carmen with similarly robust embraces.

Maribelle was the Cruz family's cook and house-keeper, but she was also a substitute grandmother for Alicia. Alicia had no idea exactly how old Maribelle was. Her hair was white in front, but jet black from the crown back. Her face was round, soft, and crinkled around her eyes and mouth, and her skin was perpet-ually tanned. To Alicia, who had never known a life without Maribelle, the woman never seemed to change.

"Have you had lunch, *niñas*?" Maribelle asked now.

"No, but we're ready to move straight to dessert," Alicia said, eyeing the freshly baked dulce de leche cake cooling on the counter. She reached down to scoop some of the chocolate icing off with her fingers and Maribelle pretended to smack her hand.

"That's for later, when your parents get home," Maribelle said with a *tsk-tsk*. "You've got to eat. How does three *cubano* sandwiches sound? I've got roast pork and manchego cheese."

Alicia smiled. "I love you, Maribelle. Thank you."

"Do you love *me*?" Maribelle teased. "Or do you love my *food*?"

"Can't I love both?"

"*Gracias*, Maribelle," Carmen said, picking up a tray of three tall, icy glasses of horchata from the counter where Maribelle had left them.

"Totes," Jamie called out, following Carmen and Alicia through the glass doors to the pool.

In the kitchen, Maribelle muttered to herself, "'Totes.' What is this 'totes'? It is hard enough keeping up with teenagers in one language, much less two."

The three girls waded into the pool, where they'd held at least a dozen Amigas Inc. meetings that summer.

It was not even noon and the temperature was well over a hundred degrees. There were only two choices in Miami on days like this: seek out the chilliest, most air-conditioned room you could find, or get into the water. Gaz's job at the Gap dictated the AC option for him; the girls had gone with the latter.

"So, what do you think of *Project Quince*?" Carmen asked as she arranged herself on a flotation pillow in the pool. She had done some more research on Mary Kenoyer's proposition when she got home from her dad's set, and now she filled her friends in on what she'd learned. The TV show Mary had mentioned was called *Project Quince*. From what Carmen could tell, it was a reality show and would showcase two different girls getting ready for their *quinces*. The girl with the best party—and party-planners—would win some pretty sweet stuff. They were also given a budget.

"Well," Alicia said when Carmen finished filling them in, "a thousand dollars isn't much of a budget."

Jamie rolled her eyes. "So says the rich girl."

Carmen stepped in to mediate before Alicia could retaliate. "Don't start. This is an amazing opportunity. If my mom and stepdad find out that the TV station is going to pay for my *quince*, no matter how little, they will be thrilled. There's a budget for my *quince*, but with six kids, things are always tight for them."

Jamie nodded, understanding. "Sometimes having a

limited budget makes you extra creative," she pointed out. "Like the way I hooked up my line of sneakers for the freestyle show. Short on cash, but long on creativity."

Alicia chimed in. "And having a Jewish fashionista *quince* is a great twist. We'd definitely stand out."

"So, we're doing it?" Carmen said. She knew her theme wasn't fleshed out yet, but they would get to that. "You *really* want to open your lives up to the camera?" It was a rhetorical question. Alicia would never back away from the opportunity—as a businesswoman *and* a TV junkie.

"We're doing it," Alicia confirmed. "*Project Quince* is on."

At that moment, Maribelle opened the patio door. "I could bring lunch outside, but it's so hot," she announced. "Better you eat inside."

The girls toweled off and made their way into the breakfast nook, where the Cruz family ate their more casual meals. The *cubano* sandwiches were lying on a plate and were hot and cheesy, which was perfect in the coolness of the air-conditioned room.

Carmen took a big bite and sighed. "Nobody makes sandwiches like Maribelle."

Alicia, who'd already finished half of her sandwich nodded. "Agreed. Speaking of which, I did some research about traditional Jewish foods, and I've been thinking that at your *quince*, we could serve noodle kugel, potato latkes, and bagels and lox."

Carmen let out a loud laugh. "We're *not* having bagels and lox at my *quince*." Then she grew silent. If only she knew what they *were* going to eat. . . .

Although the idea of having her *quince* featured on a major television show was exciting, the problem of how to have a *quinceañera* that would meld her Latin heritage and her Jewish religion was all Carmen could think about. Since she had left Alicia's house, her mind had been going about a hundred miles per hour. Now she sat up in the room she shared with her sister, anxiously playing with a piece of fabric.

"So, what do you think, *Una la Unica*," Carmen said, riffing on her sister's nickname. Legend had it that their parents had begun calling her Una because when their mother became pregnant with her brother, Tino, Una—whose birth name was Valentina—had thrown a fit and said, *"Sola una. Sola una."* In other words, that she should be their only child. It had stuck—and her wish hadn't come true.

"Think about what?" Una said as she flat-ironed her hair.

"How can I make my *quince* more Jewish?" Carmen reached into the closet and took out a set of rollers and began to set her own hair.

The two girls were wearing the same set of Victoria's Secret T-jamas. Una's was a short-sleeved lavender T-shirt with blue and purple plaid pants, and Carmen's was a white T with mint green and pink plaid pajama pants.

"You mean, how can you make *Abuela* Ruben happy?" Una asked, her gaze never wavering from the mirror, where she carefully straightened her locks, piece by piece.

"*Exactly,*" Carmen said, tucking her hair neatly around the curlers.

"You *can't* make anybody happy," Una said. "You can only please yourself."

"You sound just like Mom," Carmen moaned.

Una balled up a couple of elastics and threw them playfully at Carmen. "Shut up. I do not."

"If you say so. But seriously," Carmen went on, "I should've done like you—had a bat mitzvah and a *quince.*"

Una put the iron down and turned to look at her sister. "Do you know why I did that?"

Carmen shrugged. "Of course. Because you wanted

to honor your Jewish roots *and* your Latin heritage."

Una rolled her eyes. "No, *tonta*. I did it because that way I got twice as many presents."

Carmen gasped; she did feel a little *tonta*. "Why didn't I think of that?"

Una turned her attention back to her hair. "Because you're a Goody Two-shoes, and I'm not."

Carmen picked up the elastics to throw them back. "Do not throw things at me!" Una scolded, catching her in the act in the mirror. "I'm holding a dangerous hot instrument."

At that moment, Christian poked his head into the room. "Ah, childhood. It never changes. Someone is always throwing something; someone is always holding a dangerous hot instrument."

Carmen thought she'd never tire of Christian's British accent or his slightly goofy sense of humor. Both she and Una had agreed that when it was time for them to go to college, they were going to study abroad in England, not in Spain or Latin America, the way most Miami girls did.

"Carmen," Christian said. "Phone for you. Someone named Domingo."

Carmen leaped out of the bed. "Domingo from Bongos?"

Christian and Sophia's daughters were only six and eight years old, so his experience with being a parent of teenagers was still limited, despite the fact that he'd been married to Carmen's mother for years.

He sighed and said in his charming accent, "The young man did not say, 'Domingo from Bongos.' But I assume that if that is where you gave your phone number to someone named Domingo, then this is he."

"Who's Domingo?" Una asked, a smile playing at the corners of her mouth. She sensed an opportunity to do some serious teasing.

Carmen shot her a look that said "later" and stepped into the hallway to take the call. Grabbing the portable phone from the table in the hall, she walked onto the little Juliet balcony off the upstairs hallway. It was one of the few places in the Ramirez-Ruben house where you could really be alone.

"Hello?" she said tentatively.

"Hi," the voice on the other end of the line said. "It's Domingo, from Bongos."

Carmen looked out onto the canal and realized for the first time why they called the little space off the hallway the Juliet balcony. She was pretty sure this was exactly where you were meant to stand when your own Romeo called.

"Hey," she said, trying to play it cool. "How's it going?"

"Good," Domingo said. Then he laughed. "Aren't you going to ask me where I got your number?"

Carmen flushed and said a silent thank you that he couldn't see her. "Um, yeah, how *did* you get my number?" She tried to listen to the answer, but the voice on the other end was as smooth as milk chocolate, and all she could think was yum, yum, and, oh, yeah, yum.

There was a silence and Domingo said, "Are you still there?"

Carmen sputtered. "Yeah, um, sorry. So how'd you get my number again?"

This time, she willed herself to listen, in spite of the fact that the ducks that lived in the canal had chosen this exact moment to do their evening march and were sending out a cacophony of quacks.

"Well, you left the restaurant so quickly," Domingo said.

"Yeah, my mom was picking me up, and she hates it when I'm late."

"So, I asked your friend, the one with the cool sneaks."

"Jamie," Carmen said, making a mental note to give Jamie a big hug when she saw her.

"Yeah, her. She gave me your number and said

something about you needing to get a life," Domingo said, chuckling.

"Nice," Carmen said, making a mental note to scratch the hug and give Jamie's butt a kick when she saw her.

"I find it hard to believe that a beautiful girl like you doesn't have guys beating down her door," Domingo went on. "Are you seeing somebody?"

Carmen was once again glad that Domingo wasn't there. If he had been, he would have seen her jaw drop almost to the floor. Quickly she tried to think of something fun and witty to say. "Just you," she finally said, flirting a little harder than was her usual style.

It paid off. Domingo laughed, and Carmen was pretty sure it was the nicest sound she'd ever heard. "In that case, I should take you out on a proper date. Not just bring you free drinks when you come into Bongos. The question is when. I work at the restaurant six days a week, but I'm off on Sundays."

"Of course, you are," Carmen said. "Domingo can't work on *domingo*." She was met with silence. Now it was her turn to ask, "Are you there?"

"I'm here," Domingo answered.

"Do you get it? You're off on Sunday and your name is Domingo. It's a joke."

"I get it," he said. "Only a beautiful girl could get away with such a corny joke. I'll see you on Sunday."

They said their good-byes, but Carmen continued to stand on the balcony. She didn't want to go inside. Not yet. She wanted to hold onto this feeling. At that very moment, her life felt magical. There was no other word for it.

Finally she walked back into the hall. She didn't have time to return the cordless to the base before Tino grabbed it out of her hand.

"Nice job hogging the phone, squirt," he said.

Usually, she'd put him in his place with a quick comeback. But tonight, she had other things on her mind. She had to memorize the entire conversation so she could tell it to Una, and then to Alicia, and then to Jamie. But the words kept blurring together. All she could think about was the sound of Domingo's voice. It wasn't, she decided, like milk chocolate at all. His voice was much better. More complicated. Like dark chocolate toffee sprinkled with sea salt.

When she got back to her room, Una was waiting for her, as she had expected. Carmen was about to tell her all about the conversation when her sister spoke.

"Hey," she said, turning around. "There was something else I wanted to tell you about my bat mitzvah."

Carmen looked over, surprised.

"It wasn't all about the presents," Una said. "The one thing I really loved about my bat mitzvah was learning Hebrew."

She wadded up a piece of paper and threw it at Carmen.

"What was that for?" Carmen said, catching it.

"That's the number of my Hebrew tutor. In case you want to check it out."

Una's words brought Carmen crashing back to reality. Dream boy or not, date or not, she had a party to plan and a theme to pick out . . . and the clock was ticking.

CHAPTER 6

THE NEXT MORNING, Alicia and Carmen met at the Whip 'N' Dip, in Coral Gables. After extensive study of Miami's frozen yogurt spots, they had decided that the Whip 'N' Dip, while decidedly old-school and not as well decorated as some of the newer places, had the best fro yo in town.

When Alicia arrived, Carmen was already sitting at their favorite table outside. They played a quick round of "Red Carpet Arrivals."

Alicia held up the pretend microphone first. "Miss Ramirez-Ruben, you never fail to delight. What are you wearing?"

Carmen assumed the pigeon-toed stance that *Teen Vogue* said all the models used because it made their legs seem longer. "Well, Alicia," she replied, "I'm wearing my own label, Viva Carmen. It's a play on a mechanic's jumpsuit, except I made it in white, with red streaks, and I cut it into a short short."

Alicia nodded. "A modern take on the classics is what makes Carmen Ramirez-Ruben a red-carpet darling."

Carmen grinned. Her turn.

"We're here at the Teen Choice Awards with Miss Alicia Cruz," Carmen said. "Alicia, what are you wearing?"

Her voice was so convincing that some of the older couples at the other tables turned around to see what was going on. Something was always being filmed in Miami, so it wouldn't have been that surprising to see two stylish girls working on a TV show or film. But the onlookers quickly realized that Carmen was holding nothing in her hand but her imagination. Still, both girls continued to ham it up as if there were real cameras capturing their every move.

Alicia gave Carmen a very Hollywood air-kiss and said, in her best Salma Hayek impersonation, "Carmen, so lovely to see you. I am wearing a D&G T-shirt. My jeans are from Topshop. And the cap is from my boyfriend. He is in the navy. I also wear his boots, because I have very, very big feet."

Jamie walked up to the table just as Carmen nearly split her gut laughing.

"What are you guys doing?" she asked. "Wait, don't tell me. 'Red Carpet Arrivals.' Do you guys actually still find that fun?"

Her two friends nodded.

"Different strokes," Jamie said. "Let's order up some tasty goodness."

Carlos, the owner of Whip 'N' Dip, was an older man from Cuba who had known Alicia's parents since *they* were kids. The *amigas* were loyal to him, but that didn't stop them from campaigning for new flavors on a regular basis.

"Come on, Carlos, when are you going to make me that green tea fro yo that I've been *fiending* for?" Alicia said.

"*Y yo quiero lichis,*" Carmen added.

"And what about pomegranate?" Jamie said. "Every fro yo store in New York has pomegranate."

Carlos shook his head and, in a tone of mock frustration, pointed to his wares. "No, *sabe, aquí, nos gustan los originales.* We've got coconut, mango, pineapple, banana, strawberry. It's not enough for you, then you no whip it or dip it."

"We know, we know," Alicia said. "Banana whip in a cup with chocolate shavings, *por favor.*"

"*Piña* on a stick, frozen," Carmen said. "*Gracias,* Señor Carlos."

"Coconut whip in a cup, thanks," ordered Jamie.

• • •

Back outside, with frozen treats in hand, the girls sat down at their table.

"I've got something to tell you," Carmen said, her words coming out in a rush. She was too pumped to keep her news inside any longer.

"Me, too!" Jamie cried.

"Well, mine involves a really cute new boy," Carmen chimed in.

Jamie shrugged. "As mine involves a wicked shipment of Bathing Ape T-shirts from Osaka, I think you can go first," she said, admitting defeat.

"Remember the waiter from Bongos the other day?" Carmen asked.

Jamie raised an eyebrow playfully. She knew where this was going. "The MWAH?"

"That would be the one," Carmen said. "His name is Domingo, and we're going out on Sunday."

Alicia giggled. "You're going out with Domingo on *domingo*? That's funny."

Carmen beamed. "I know! That's what I said. He didn't think it was quite as funny."

"You're smooth, *chica*," Alicia said. "I didn't even see you two exchange numbers."

"Of course you didn't," Jamie said proudly. "Because *I* gave him Carmen's number."

"Indeed she did. And by the way, *gracias, chica,*" Carmen said, reaching out to give Jamie a high five.

"Girl's got your back!" Alicia said.

"*Claro,*" Carmen said, biting into her frozen yogurt pop. "That's only part of my news."

"There's more?" Alicia asked.

"Even better. Well, maybe not better . . . but just as fantastic. Someone from Channel Six news called to say that Sharon Kim wants us to come in to the station tomorrow to discuss *Project Quince*—maybe on air!"

Alicia nearly choked on her fro yo. "Tomorrow? As in day after today? But my hair is a mess and I need to get a manicure, and . . ."

"Whoa, chill, *chica,*" Jamie said. "We'll probably be on air for like, five seconds. Plus, you gotta get used to this. *Project Quince* is a *show,* after all."

Carmen laughed at Alicia's now frozen expression. "Jamie's right, Lici. This is just a quick thing. Then we'll hear more about the show. So no freaking out. What's the worst that could happen?"

The next morning, Carmen, Alicia, Gaz, and Jamie arrived at the television station to meet with Sharon Kim and Mary Kenoyer, the producer who had approached

Carmen. This was their big break, and each of them knew it. They'd all gotten there more than half an hour early. And despite the assurances yesterday that this was not a freak-out moment, they'd each dressed to impress. Jamie, the quintessential B-boy, ramped it up in a black strapless jumpsuit and, very uncharacteristically, a long strand of pearls.

Alicia raised an eyebrow. "For real?"

Jamie responded, "I saw this movie about Coco Chanel the other night, and what can I say? I was inspired. I borrowed these from my mom."

"You certainly are rocking them," Carmen said, nodding appreciatively.

"And you're nothing if not versatile," Alicia added.

Jamie did a little spin. "Thanks. So, let's do this!"

Walking into the television studio, the friends fell silent as they took in the pictures of all the faces they'd watched onscreen over the years. The receptionist, who looked old enough to have invented TV, squawked, "Do you have a purpose being here? This is not a museum. You can't just come in and look at the pictures."

"Why does it got to be like that?" Jamie mumbled.

"Because we're teenagers," Carmen replied, calmly.

"Because we're Latin," Jamie retorted.

Ever the leader, Alicia stepped forward. "We have a

ten a.m. appointment with Sharon Kim."

The receptionist looked haughtily at Alicia. "And you are . . . ?"

"Amigas Incorporated," Alicia answered smoothly. "She's expecting us."

The receptionist made a call. After a few moments, she directed the four to go through the door behind her. "Straight down that hall, take the elevator to the third floor," she droned in a nasal voice. "Have a nice day."

The moment the door closed behind them, Jamie started to fume. "Have a nice day? Have a nice day?"

Alicia took a deep breath and held up a hand. "Would Coco Chanel let this get to her?"

Jamie sighed. "I guess not."

Carmen smiled and, in the dulcet tones of an inspirational speaker, said, "*Be* the pearls."

Jamie scowled. "This is why I don't wear pearls."

Unfortunately, the receptionist wasn't the worst thing they were going to see that day. And Carmen's promise of nothing bad happening proved to be wrong. To say that they were surprised to see Simone Baldonado standing in the office with Sharon and Mary would have been an understatement.

"Hello, commoners," Simone said, clearly relishing

their discomfort as they entered.

Alicia turned to the TV producer. "No offense, but she's not part of Amigas Incorporated. What is she doing here?"

Mary smiled. "I'm sorry if I didn't make this clear when I spoke with Carmen. *Project Quince* is a *competition*. Two teams. One goal: who can throw the most innovative *quince* for a thousand dollars or less? The prize is three thousand dollars that can go to the *quince*'s party or whatever you choose. In addition, you and Simone's team will battle it out in a series of three different impromptu challenges for the pilot episode. If the show is successful, then we'll have two groups of *chicas* go at it every month for a year. You are, in effect, guinea pigs."

When Mary was done speaking, Alicia smoothed an invisible wrinkle on her shirt. "Excuse me. Can we just have a moment?"

As soon as they stepped into the hall, Alicia's composure broke and she frowned. "I know this is an amazing opportunity, but I'm not down with Simone being part of it. Nothing is ever easy—or fair—when she's involved."

Gaz straightened his tie. "We'll crush her," he said, looking serious.

"We've built this business out of nothing," Carmen added with a confident nod. "We can handle Simone."

Jamie nodded, too. "It's worth it for all that loot. We can use the prize money for our trip to New York."

Alicia knew when she was outnumbered. "Okay, so we're in," she said with renewed determination as they walked back into the office. "But we do have some concerns."

"That's great," Mary said. "Now, if you don't mind, Jamie, our sound tech will mike you."

"Even for this first meeting?" Alicia asked.

Sharon beamed. "We don't want to miss a thing! We'll need all of you to sign releases, and, because you're minors, your parents will have to sign, too. That's why we decided this discussion wouldn't be aired live. But let's go ahead and get you miked up for future material. Simone already has hers on."

Alicia and Carmen exchanged glances as the sound technician handed them the mikes to slip inside their shirts, then deftly clipped the mikes to the backs of their outfits. The reality of the situation finally hit home. All those years of playing "Red Carpet Arrivals," and now they were going to be on an honest-to-goodness TV show. It didn't seem possible.

Jamie did Alicia, then Carmen, then herself. When

Jamie was done, she turned to Sharon and said, "Okay, good to go."

Sharon shot them one of her trademark bright sunny smiles with which she managed to report about even the most bizarre news ("Crocodile saves infant baby; baby unharmed! News at eleven!"). "We're listening now, to all of you," she said. "These microphones are extremely sensitive. So, watch your mumbling. And watch your language! Remember, this is a family television station!"

They all sat down around a conference table. "Now, as you have mentioned, Alicia, I believe you have some concerns. I feel it would be best to hear them before we get too involved in the show."

"I agree. I—we—only have one concern, really— Simone doesn't do *quinces*. She's got a Sweet *Sixteen* business," Alicia said, speaking to Sharon and ignoring Simone. "A brand-new business," she added under her breath.

Sharon raised a perfectly sculpted eyebrow. "That *is* a problem, because the show is called *Project Quince*. MTV already has *My Super Sweet 16*. Simone, you informed us you did *quinceañeras*."

Simone made a face. "I *do* do *quinces*. I'm . . . um . . . doing Raymunda Itoi's in a month."

"Raymunda?" Jamie said. "Who's that? I don't know any Raymunda at Coral Gables."

Simone flipped her hair back over her shoulder. "That's right, you don't," she said, her voice icy. "Because she's a Brazilian Japanese girl from Hialeah High."

"Simone, we've worked hard to make our business work," Alicia said, unable to hold back. "Why are you stepping up like this?"

"Like you need the money," Simone said. "Exploiting poor Latina girls for their last peso when you could afford to help them for free."

"Um, pot calling the kettle black?" Alicia growled.

"*My* family has been in the hospitality business for *years*," Simone said.

"Then why aren't you more freakin' hospitable?" Alicia asked.

The girls argued back and forth, unaware that Sharon's cameraman had started filming them. It was only when Sharon began clapping that Alicia bit her tongue. This was not the impression she wanted to make.

"You know what, just forget it," Alicia said, lowering her voice.

"No! Don't forget it. Keep going!" Sharon said, gesturing to Simone and Alicia to get back in each other's faces. "This is great drama for the show!"

Watching the antics, Carmen, Jamie, and Gaz exchanged looks. What had they gotten themselves into?

CHAPTER 7

CARMEN WOKE up Sunday morning at six. Between thoughts of the TV show and her upcoming date, she was a wreck.

Domingo was picking her up at noon, but she had a lot to do beforehand. The night before, he had called to confirm the date and told her to pack a swimsuit. But he wouldn't tell her where they were going. In Miami, telling someone to pack a swimsuit was hardly a clue. There was water *everywhere*. If they were going to South Beach, Carmen would need to pack a bikini—the less material, the better. If they were going to Coconut Grove, she'd definitely want to bring her sarong and a pair of jeweled flip-flops, because the vibe there was more stylish, more grown-up. The Nikki Beach Club was ground zero for the Beautiful People. If they were going there, Carmen would need much more than a swimsuit. She'd need a whole poolside *ensemble*: hoop earrings, stiletto heels, a big necklace . . .

By the time Una woke up, Carmen had been laying outfits on her bed, mixing and matching (no greater crime than being matchy-matchy) for two hours.

Una rolled over, her curls tousled and beautiful as always. "Ugh, stop making so much noise! What are you doing?"

Carmen had already showered—hot water being always in short supply in their full house—and was dressed in a short summer robe.

"I'm getting ready for my date with Domingo," Carmen said.

"Right," Una quipped. "Domingo on *domingo*."

Carmen scowled. "For some reason, he doesn't find that funny. So don't mention it when you meet him."

Una shook her head. "I won't meet him. I've got dance-team practice at ten a.m. I'll be long gone. What's with all of this? I thought you were going to the beach."

"We *are*," Carmen said. "I just don't know which beach. And you know, every beach and pool club has its own style."

Una threw her head back in mock frustration. "Doesn't matter. There only one foolproof beach-date outfit."

She got out of bed, reached into her own drawer, and pulled out a coral tankini, a white lace minidress, and a coral and white bandanna.

"This is what I should wear?" Carmen asked, bewildered. "But you never let me borrow your clothes. You always say I'm going to ruin them."

"Stop talking!" Una ordered. "And start listening. Like I said, there's only one foolproof beach-date outfit."

Carmen sat on her desk chair and listened.

"Tankini on the first date," Una went on. "Even if you have ripped abs like mine and legs that go on forever, like yours, you are a nice girl. Show it by *not* showing it. A tankini is cute and sporty. Guys don't love them, but they shouldn't get everything they want out of life. Especially on the first date. Do you understand what I'm saying?"

Carmen blushed. Was her sister actually talking to her about sex? As if. She wasn't even fifteen yet.

"Pay attention!" Una snapped. "I'm not speaking for my health. The tankini should be in a nice soft color. Girls usually like bold colors like black and turquoise and red. Guys tend to go for pastels. You compromise with coral and it shows off the brown in our natural skin tone."

"Okay," Carmen said, smiling. She kind of loved

it when her big sister got bossy.

"The white lace minidress is an American classic," Una said. "Look at Ali MacGraw. Look at Sienna Miller. Look at decades of actresses who know style. It's a little dressy, but not too dressy. Also, if you spill something on it, no sweat—you just bleach it out."

"What about the scarf?" Carmen asked.

"After you swim, don't even bother trying to blow-dry your hair in a public restroom," Una explained. "Shampoo it; run your fingers through it. Fold the scarf in half and wear your hair loose underneath it. It's casual, it's chic. And this scarf is vintage Pucci, so you lose it and I'll kill you."

Carmen jumped up to give her sister a big hug.

"Save the gratitude," Una said. "I'm not done. The jeweled flip-flops are the only thing you got right. Wear those."

Carmen beamed.

Una put her arms out. "Okay, I'm ready now for all that little-sister adoration and love."

Carmen smiled. "Thanks Una. You are the absolute best big sister ever."

"No worries," Una said. "Besides, he might be taking you to a place where people know me. I can't have you reflecting badly on me."

• • •

Domingo rang the doorbell at twelve o'clock on the dot. Carmen looked through the peephole and nearly lost it. He was cuter than she'd remembered.

She opened the door. "Hi."

Then Lindsay popped up out of nowhere. "Hi," she said, parroting her big sister.

Domingo smiled. "Well, hello to both of you."

Lindsay was quickly followed by the twins, who were learning Spanish. They stuck their little blond heads out from behind the door and said, *"Hola."*

"Hello, there, to you, too," Domingo said good-naturedly.

They stood there for a second until Domingo finally said, "Ummm, are you going to ask me in?"

Carmen giggled nervously. "Oh, yeah, of course," she said. "Come in."

Shooing the younger girls away she led him to the back of the house. Sophia and Christian were working in the backyard garden, as was their habit on Sunday mornings.

"Hey, you guys," Carmen said. "This is Domingo."

"Well, Domingo, it's a pleasure," Sophia said, taking off her gardening gloves to shake his hand. "I have to admit, I don't really need gloves to tend to the basil and mint plants in our little herb garden. But I enjoy the accoutrements of gardening as much as I enjoy the work."

"Nice to meet you ma'am," Domingo said, the picture of politeness.

Christian wiped his hands on his jeans and then shook Domingo's hand heartily. "You will have her home by three, won't you?"

Domingo looked confused. "Three in the morning?"

Christian pretended to be annoyed. "Come on, what are you playing at? Three in the afternoon. We run a tight ship around here, you know."

Domingo looked seriously worried.

Carmen laughed. "Ignore him, please."

"Please do," Christian added. "I'm just taking the piss."

"Excuse me?" Domingo said.

"Sorry, it's confusing. Taking the piss is British for making fun of you," Carmen explained.

"Right." Domingo nodded, a little uncertain.

"Have a good time," Sophia called out, returning to her gardening. She hit Christian on the shoulder with her gardening gloves. "Don't worry about this one."

"No, seriously," Christian said. "See you at six, Carmen?"

"How about seven?" she replied.

"Seven's fine," Christian said.

When they finally escaped and walked outside, Carmen was in for a surprise. Sharon, Mary, and Arnie, the cameraman they'd been introduced to briefly at the station, were waiting for them. She had completely forgotten about the show!

"We just need you to sign this," Mary said, handing Domingo a piece of paper.

"What's this?" he asked, looking confused. "Are we being punked?"

Carmen looked around, hoping the ground might open up and swallow her whole. She took a deep breath and said, "No, nothing like that. I'm being filmed for this *quinceañera* competition. They get to follow me everywhere."

"It's part of the deal," Sharon said, sunnily.

"Okay," Domingo said, as he signed his name. "I'll agree. But with limits. You can film us going to the car and no further."

"Great," Mary said, taking the release. "Now, we just need to mike you for sound."

"The car and no further," Domingo repeated.

"Yes, yes, we understand. Now, pretend like we're not here," Mary said.

Carmen and Domingo began to walk past the canals

to where his car was parked. Carmen saw him taking in the riverside neighborhood—the sky-high palm trees, the painted boats, the arch of the bridge, the soft breeze as the water in the canal whistled by. Walking next to him, she felt as if she were seeing it all with fresh eyes herself. It was a little odd to be followed by the camera crew, but maybe the longer they hung around, the easier it would be to ignore them.

"So where did you two meet?" Sharon called out.

Or maybe not, Carmen thought.

"At Bongos Café," Domingo replied over his shoulder.

"And this is your first date?" Sharon asked.

"Yep," Carmen said.

"And are you going to be Carmen's date for her *quince*?" Sharon asked.

"It's hard to act like you're not there if you keep talking," Domingo said, trying to appear good-natured.

"You're absolutely right," Sharon agreed.

"Yep, fall back, team," Mary said.

The entire camera crew took a dozen steps back, and Carmen could feel her shoulders relaxing. It was nice to see Domingo stand up for her; it made her feel protected.

"It's so beautiful back here," Domingo said, turning

the topic away from show-inspired questions. "It's like a secret tropical garden."

Carmen smiled. "Funny you should say that. My friend Alicia—you met her at Bongos—says the same thing. When we were kids, that was the name of our favorite book: *The Secret Garden.* I always thought the woman who'd written it could have lived here. Speaking of secrets, where are we going?"

Now it was Domingo's turn to smile. "You'll see."

When they arrived at the car, Domingo held up a hand. "Good-bye, television people."

"Could you tell us where you're going?" Mary asked.

"And risk you horning in on our date? I don't think so," Domingo said, grinning.

"Could we get a kiss for the camera?" Sharon asked in a playful tone.

"The kiss comes after the date," Domingo said.

"Hasta luego," Carmen said, waving.

Making a quick getaway, they drove along Collins Avenue, the ocean glimmering at their right the entire way.

"It's nice to finally be alone with you," Domingo said.

"Ditto," Carmen replied.

They were quiet as they admired the scenery.

Carmen never got tired of it. She couldn't imagine a more beautiful place to live than Miami, except maybe for Hawaii. She'd seen pictures and it seemed a lot like Miami, except that in place of all the skyscrapers and city streets, there were mountains and volcanos and water in every direction.

"So, what's it like at Hialeah High?" Carmen asked when the silence had gone on long enough. He had mentioned, when he had called to confirm their plans, that that was where he went.

Domingo shrugged. "It's cool. It's not as fancy as C. G. High, but we have a lot of fun."

"What's your favorite subject?" Carmen asked.

"English," Domingo said. "I know it sounds nerdy, but I love to read. I took this class in Latin American fiction last year and it just about blew my mind."

Carmen smiled. "Nerdy is good. Trust me. I'm nerdy too—especially with things like music. Speaking of which, what are we listening to?"

"Wilco," Domingo said. "Do you like it?"

"I like anything new," Carmen said. "So . . . where are we going?"

"*Paciencia, niña,*" Domingo said. "We're almost there."

Carmen laughed. "Nice move, breaking out the

Spanish to avoid answering. Are you fluent?"

Domingo shook his head. "Nah. I speak kindergarten Spanish."

"What's that?" Carmen asked.

"You know, the stuff your mom tells you again and again when you're five. 'Slow down.' 'Close your mouth.' 'Go to sleep.' 'Come, eat.' 'Don't eat so fast.'"

Carmen nodded.

"Are you fluent?" Domingo asked.

"Nah," Carmen said. "I guess I speak kindergarten Spanish, too. Plus a little fashion Spanish, because I design and make clothes. Oh, and, I speak a little Ladino."

"What's that?" Domingo asked.

"It's this Sephardic-Latino tradition. My dad's family is from Argentina, and every spring, my grandmother comes up from Buenos Aires to cook us Passover seder and we sing these *Coplas de Purim en español*."

"Well, *vaya*, sing me one."

Carmen shook her head. "No way! I can't embarrass myself this early on our first date!"

"Well, you're lucky, 'cause I'm letting you off the hook—for now," Domingo said. "We're here."

Carmen shifted her gaze forward and saw they had pulled into the driveway of the Loews. It was one of the swanky hotels right on Miami Beach.

Carmen could feel her chest tightening. Wait a second. Hotels had rooms, and rooms had beds. What did Domingo have in mind? This was a first date, after all!

She must have looked as terrified as she felt, because Domingo spoke up. "I have a friend who works at the pool. I thought we'd hang out there."

Carmen was so relieved she almost hugged him.

Domingo took a large picnic basket out of the trunk of his car.

"What's that?" she asked.

He winked at her. "Lunch."

They went through the opulent lobby and out to the pool. Quickly they settled in at a poolside cabana, which normally cost $500 a day, though Domingo's friend, Santiago, was letting them have it for free. The cabana was yellow and white and was as big as Carmen's living room. It had a small bistro table with two chairs, an upholstered chaise longue, a TV, and a fridge stocked with bottled water.

Domingo stepped out while Carmen changed into her bathing suit, and when he returned he laid out lunch.

"I tried to remember all your favorites," he said. "But I was only your waiter once."

Carmen blushed as he began pulling containers out of the basket.

"Stuffed green plantain chips with shrimp creole?"

"Yum," Carmen said.

"Fried plantains with garlic sauce?"

"Double yum."

"*Papas rellenas?*"

"Uh, I think that's a—yum."

"And virgin *mojitos* in a not-so-attractive thermos," Domingo finished.

"It's perfect. It's more than perfect. This may just be the sweetest thing anyone's ever done for me," Carmen said.

Without stopping to think about what she was doing, she leaned over and kissed him lightly on the lips. "Now that's over with and we can relax, instead of there being all that tension later when you take me home."

"That's a very interesting theory," Domingo said, smiling. "I like it."

"Good," Carmen said. "Because I like you. And I'd like to kiss you a lot."

"I guess it's a good thing I sent those television people away," Domingo said.

Carmen laughed—and kissed him again.

• • •

The minute Carmen got home, the first thing she did was call Alicia to tell her all about the date.

Alicia sighed. "Will you still be my best friend if I tell you that I'm just a little bit jealous of you right now?"

Carmen laughed giddily. *"Claro."*

"What if I told you I was *really, really* jealous of you right now?"

"But why?" Carmen said. "You've got Gaz."

"Gaz doesn't make me picnics or take me to a poolside cabana," Alicia said.

"Maybe he would if you'd admit he was really your boyfriend," Carmen advised, her voice softening.

Alicia took a deep breath. "I have to ask," she said, "did he kiss you good-bye?"

Carmen nodded, as though Alicia could see her over the phone. "Yes, he did."

Alicia inhaled sharply. "Okay, now I'm just being nosy, but I have to know. We're talking a full kiss, with tongue, right?"

"Uh, yeah. That's what girls and boys who aren't in 'flirtationships' do, Lici. You should try it. It's nice."

Alicia was quiet for a little bit, and Carmen began to worry that perhaps she'd offended her friend.

"Are you there, Lici?" Carmen said. "I didn't mean to be rude."

"I'm here," Alicia said. "It's just this whole thing with Gaz and me. I've never had a real boyfriend before. I don't want to mess things up. I can't have my first relationship with someone who's also one of my best friends."

"Why not?" Carmen asked. "Isn't the friend bit the most important part of 'boyfriend'?"

After the phone call with Alicia, eating dinner with the family, and doing the dishes, Carmen finally walked into her bedroom to find her sister engaged in the nightly ritual of moisturizing.

"Hey, Una," she said. "Thanks for hooking me up today."

"Did you have a nice time?" her sister asked, staring straight ahead into the mirror.

"I did."

"Mom and Christian seemed to really like him," Una said. "Mom said he'll make the most handsome *chambelán* Miami has ever seen."

Carmen laughed. "That's funny. That's exactly what Alicia said."

"Even a blind person could see that he's your *bashert*," Una said, smiling.

"What's that?" Carmen said. "I haven't started

Hebrew lessons yet you know."

"Your *bashert* is your destiny in love. It means he's the one."

Carmen felt a funny stirring inside, like the faintest of flutters. Una's words made sense. Even though Carmen had been out with Domingo only once and had kissed him only a few times that day, there was a sense of peace about it all. It was as though, with every kiss, she had felt more certain that something amazing was happening. Her sister might just be right. Maybe Domingo was the one.

CHAPTER 8

EARLY THE next morning, Alicia knocked on the door of Carmen's house. "Come on," she said when her friend opened the door. "Let's go for a little boat ride."

Carmen groaned. "It's so early. I'm still in my pajamas."

Alicia, who was dressed in a Topshop bubble dress with gray and white ticking, didn't care. "No biggie, you're wearing a cami and sweatpants. No one will know you slept in that!"

Carmen put her hand up to her mouth. "I haven't brushed my teeth."

Alicia paused, then said, "*Mejores amigas o no*, it might be a good idea if you did that."

A few minutes later, Carmen emerged—teeth brushed, hair pulled back into a ponytail, and a dab of lip gloss on her lips.

"Makeup, *niña*?" Alicia said.

"Don't hate!" Carmen teased. "You're showered—and fully dressed."

They made their way to the boat and quickly got in. Alicia was apparently making up for all the time she had let pass without being on the water. Carmen began to row them toward the bridge.

"What's so urgent that it couldn't wait?" Carmen said, watching the parade of ducks take their morning exercise.

"First, I got you breakfast," Alicia said, holding up a bag Carmen hadn't noticed in her sleepy state. "Empanadas and iced Cuban coffee."

"*Gracias.* I'm starving!" Carmen put down the oars to eat. "So, tell me. What's up?" she asked after she swallowed a big bite of the tasty treat.

Alicia reached into her bag. "I've solved all of your problems. I spent all day yesterday at the Jewish Cultural Center in Aventura, and look what I found."

She took out a book and handed it to Carmen.

Carmen looked at it. "*Tropical Synagogue*?" she read, sounding confused.

"*Tropical Synagogue*," Alicia repeated. "It's a collection of writing by Jewish Latino writers."

"Great," Carmen said. "But how does that solve my problems?"

Alicia smiled. "That's why I wanted to come out on the boat. Turn it back around so it faces your house."

Carmen maneuvered the oars so that the little boat turned around.

"Okay, there it is," she said, putting down the oars. "My house." From where they sat it looked small and unimpressive.

Alicia smiled mischievously. "Maybe you should take some Bible study along with those Hebrew classes you're starting, ye of little faith. This is going to rock."

Carmen folded her arms, waiting.

"All right, all right. I'll tell you," Alicia said, laughing. "You know how every fall, there are the big fashion shows in the tents in New York?"

Carmen sighed. "Of course. Style.com was the first iPhone app I ever purchased."

Alicia nodded. "Picture a Fashion Week tent behind your house, facing the water."

"But I've already told you," Carmen protested, "I don't want to do a fashion-themed *quince*. I want to honor my Jewish heritage."

Alicia pulled out her iPhone. "But the tent is not just about fashion; it's a powerful symbol in Jewish literature. Check this out: I did a lot of research online, and it all mentions that the tent is a symbol found in rituals throughout all periods of Jewish history. For example, the Tent of the Tabernacle was Judaism's sacred first tent. And Jewish couples get married under a minitent open on all sides, called a chuppah."

Carmen's eyes widened. "*Abuela* Ruben would love that."

Alicia went on. "So your theme is Tropical Synagogue. The tent symbolizes both New York Fashion Week *and* a more serious form of worship and Jewish tradition. We make a runway that comes out from your back door and goes down to the water. You design some clothes. We do a fashion show, and then the runway converts into the dance floor. We line the outer perimeter of the tent with potted palm trees. That gardening shop still owes us a favor for the big account we brought them, and we fixed it when they messed up and brought calla lilies instead of Casablanca lilies. They can lend us a couple dozen palm trees. Can you picture it, C.? A big white tent, the green of the palm trees, the canal glistening in the background . . ."

"No church?" Carmen said.

Alicia shook her head. "Not for this *quince*. The tent is a portable place of worship. The symbolic, spiritual home."

Carmen flipped through the book, warming up to the idea. "What if we had Jamie graffiti the inside of the tent with excerpts from all these Jewish Latino writers?"

Alicia nodded. "That would be hot."

Carmen's smile faltered. Something had just occurred to her. "Do you really think I could mount a whole fashion show? I've got, like, a month to design and make all those outfits. Even a capsule collection with twelve looks would be nearly impossible to do."

"What would Heidi Klum and Tim Gunn say if you were on *Project Runway*?" Alicia asked.

"You know," Carmen said, sheepishly. "You've watched all the seasons on DVD with me."

"But I can't remember," Alicia said, feigning amnesia. "When some up-and-coming designer starts complaining that her fingers hurt from sewing and she didn't get the material she wanted in the challenge and the silly cat ate her pattern, what is it that Heidi and Tim say? I really just cannot remember."

Carmen crossed her arms and leaned over, staring at the bottom of the boat. Then she whispered, "They say, 'Make it work.'"

Alicia grinned. "I'm sorry. I can't hear you. What do they say?"

Carmen spoke a little louder. "Make it work."

Alicia screamed, "I can't hear you!"

Finally Carmen threw her hands in the air. "Make it work! Make it work! That's what I'm going to do.

Tropical Synagogue, baby. I'm about to make it work."

They were both still laughing as they rowed back to Carmen's house. Then they saw Sharon and Mary waiting for them and their smiles faded.

"You guys," Carmen moaned. "I'm in my pajamas. What's so important you have to be here *this* early?"

"Better get dressed quick," Sharon said. "We have a surprise for you. It's time for the first challenge! The audience is just going to love it!"

Mary nodded. "We can't tell you what it is exactly yet. But it's happening at one of Miami's top restaurants, Michy's. I hope you girls can cook!"

The two friends exchanged glances. This was going to be huge. Racing toward the house, Alicia quickly shot the rest of the group a text filling them in.

"This is bananas," Alicia said, as she followed her best friend into her room.

"Bananas, but kind of fun," Carmen agreed as she dashed into the bathroom. It was time for the quickest shower ever.

"Good thing you can cook! Gaz has work, and Jamie and I are hopeless. I'm pretty sure I can burn water," Alicia called out from behind the closed door. "What are you going to make?"

"You mean, what are *we* going to make? Burned

water or not, we are in this together," Carmen said, emerging from the bathroom in a pair of white jeans and a white necklace T-shirt that she'd made herself, attaching strands of thrift-store rhinestones to the neckline. She was dressed to win.

The *Project Quince* crew drove Carmen and Alicia to Donald's Cornucopia, a gourmet grocery store near Michy's. Jamie arrived just as they got there.

As Sharon began to explain the rules to the girls, the cameraman, Arnie, filmed them.

All three of the girls were surprised to see that, as amazing as she was on TV, even Sharon flubbed her lines on occasion.

"I'm here with Carmen Romero. . . ." the anchor began. "That's not right, let's go again."

"Sharon Kim here with one of the contestants of *Project Quinte*—I mean, *Quince*."

Even when she made mistakes, Sharon kept her cool. Carmen, on the other hand? Not so much. She tried not to blush as a small crowd gathered outside the grocery store to view what was going on.

Finally, the television personality got her lines right. "Sharon Kim here," she said, "with Carmen Ramirez-Ruben and Amigas Incorporated, one of the two teams in our first-ever *Project Quince* competition. Today's contest is all about culture. Which *quinceañera* planners can cook the most delicious Nuevo Latino dish to be served as their party's culinary centerpiece. You'll have thirty dollars and thirty minutes to shop; then we're off to Michy's for cooking and judging."

"Where's the other team?" Carmen asked, looking around.

"You mean Simone's?" Sharon asked. "She called to say that her client, Raymunda, needed some special Japanese ingredients for their dish. They'll meet us at the restaurant. But stop wasting time." She looked down at her watch. "You've got twenty-nine minutes to shop!"

Carmen took the money and the girls dashed into the grocery store, unsure of where to begin. Carmen ran to the vegetable section and grabbed several heirloom tomatoes that looked fresh, but then she heard Alicia call out, "Start with the protein!" So she ran to the meat section, with the cameraman following right behind her. It was odd having a person track her every move. She wondered if this was what it was like to be an actress in a movie or to be stalked by the paparazzi.

The minute she got to the meat counter, inspiration struck and she knew exactly what she would make:

steak with red and green chimichurri sauce. She bought a steak she hoped was big enough, told the others what she had in mind, and then heard Sharon call out, "Twenty minutes to go!"

Carmen, Alicia, and Jamie dashed around the store looking for the rest of the ingredients they needed: parsley, garlic, olive oil, white vinegar, red pepper flakes, cumin, fresh lemon, bay leaves, and paprika. They ran back and forth, from the aisles that stocked spices to the produce section to look for ingredients to round out the meal.

"Five minutes!" Sharon cried.

"Go and pay!" Alicia yelled.

There was no waiting in line, because all of the shoppers had stepped aside in order to watch the girl's mad dash.

The cashier added all of the groceries up. "Your total is $32.07."

"No can do," Sharon said. "It's got to be under thirty dollars."

Carmen made a quick decision and handed two items back to the cashier. "I don't need the rice and beans."

"Brave decision to do a Latino dish without rice and beans," Sharon said, splitting her attention evenly between the camera and Carmen.

But Carmen just smiled. "That's what makes it *Nuevo*."

At Michy's, the girls met the chef and owner, Michelle Bernstein. Michelle was like the cool older cousin you always wanted to hang out with. In a classic chef's uniform, a white coat with her name embroidered on it, jeans, and purple Crocs, the woman radiated cool. Her wavy blond ponytail made her seem way younger than she was.

"So, I hear we have something in common," Michelle said, shaking Carmen's hand. "We're both Jewish Latinas."

"Really? That's so wild," Carmen said. Outside of her immediate family and a few family friends, she didn't really know anyone who shared the same cultural roots. But before she could ask Michelle any of the dozens of questions that flashed through her mind, the cameras were rolling again.

"We are here at one of South Florida's finest restaurants, Michy's, for the first competition of *Project Quince*," Sharon said. "Our two *quinces* will have exactly one hour to prepare a dish that shows off their *Nuevo* Latino flair. James Beard Award–winning chef Michelle Bernstein will judge the dishes."

Turning to Carmen, Sharon went on. "Our first

contestants are Carmen Ramirez-Ruben and her sous-chefs, Alicia Cruz and Jamie Sosa, from Amigas Inc. What are you making today?"

Carmen took a deep breath and tried to ignore the camera. She wanted to look as natural as possible. "I'm making steak with two chimichurri sauces and a red-chili-pepper glaze."

"Sounds delicious," Sharon said. "Now, our second contestants should be here somewhere."

Sharon looked around, and from the back of the kitchen, Simone emerged with a girl dressed in a black ninja costume.

"Ah, yes. This is Raymunda Itoi," Sharon said, gesturing toward the masked figure. "And her planner, Simone Baldonado. Raymunda, can you explain your outfit? And the dish you two will be making today?"

Raymunda whispered something to Simone.

"She's very self-conscious about her accent and would like for me to speak for her while she continues to work on her English," Simone said.

Sharon looked at Mary, who gave her a thumbs-up.

"Well, my producer says it's okay," Sharon said. "So, what are you and Raymunda making?"

Simone beamed at the camera. "Florida is the gateway to Latin America, just as Japan is the gateway to

Asia, so our dish is a sashimi and ceviche platter."

Sharon looked impressed. "That sounds delicious. And what a well-thought-out concept!"

The members of Amigas Inc. looked at one another nervously.

"Okay, teams, it's time to start cooking!" Sharon said. "Aprons on. Knives up. Go!"

At first, Carmen found it hard not to keep staring at Raymunda, who seemed perfectly comfortable cooking in what looked like a Halloween costume. She was also rattled by the intense camera scrutiny. But soon Carmen settled into a groove. She had learned how to make chimichurri sauce when she was a little girl, visiting her grandmother in Buenos Aires, and could make it in her sleep. It would be no problem making it in a fancy kitchen, even with a TV camera following her around as Simone stood next to a ninja slicing and dicing raw fish just a few feet away. Plus, she had her sous-chefs. Before she knew it, she was plating her steaks and pouring the red-pepper sauce, and the time was up.

Carmen's dish was judged first by Sharon Kim, Mary Kenoyer, and Michelle Bernstein.

"Tell me about the two chimichurri sauces," Michelle said when Carmen placed the plate in front of her.

"Traditionally, chimichurri is green; it's got all the

fresh herbs in it," she explained. "But my mom, who's from Mexico, likes a chunky tomato sauce, so I started exploring how I could bring that green flavor into a red sauce."

"It's delicious," Mary said, taking a bite.

"You've done a really wonderful job," Michelle said. "The steak isn't overcooked, which is an easy mistake to make."

"I like the glaze," Sharon added.

"All around, an excellent dish," Michelle said. "Do you want to come and work for me?"

"Maybe," Carmen said, a huge smile on her face, "but it's a package deal." She nodded at her two BFs.

"Thank you to the first team. Next up are Raymunda and Simone," Sharon said.

The girl in the ninja costume handed out platters of ceviche and sashimi to the three judges as Simone posed for the cameras.

The judges had taken only a bite of the dish when Michelle spat the food into her napkin.

"Your ceviche is not cooked," she said. "If you only have an hour, you have to blanch it first. Fish cut into thick cubes will not cook in lemon juice so quickly; it's disgusting."

"The sashimi is okay," Mary said hopefully.

Michelle took a bite. "For a supermarket maybe, because I'm pretty sure that's where this came from. Overall, this is an extraordinarily disappointing dish."

"This isn't fair," Simone argued, her face a rather disturbing shade of red. "Maybe this is how Japanese people like ceviche and sushi."

Michelle shook her head. "That's just ridiculous. Good food is good food. Like you said, both Florida and Japan are gateways. Unfortunately, your dish is a gateway to food poisoning. Carmen and Amigas Inc. win."

The three girls squealed and clapped loudly.

Carmen could not wipe the huge grin off her face as she asked, "What do we win?"

"Michy's will be catering your *quinceañera* free of charge," Sharon replied. "Congratulations, girls. This will surely help make your budget stretch much further."

"No way! You've got to be kidding me!" Carmen began jumping up and down. "Thank you so much!"

"Thank *you*. It was a wonderful dish," Michelle said, shaking her hand and then moving on to congratulate Jamie and Alicia.

The chef then went over to shake Raymunda's hand. "Better luck next time," she said.

But Raymunda did not answer. She simply

unsheathed her ninja sword and pretended to commit hari-kari.

"Did you get that on film?" Mary cried out to Arnie. When it turned out he had not, she said, "Raymunda, do it again!"

Hamming it up for the cameras, Raymunda pretended to stab herself with the sword once again.

Show business, as it turned out, was brutal.

CHAPTER 9

IT WASN'T UNTIL the following Saturday morning, that Carmen, Alicia, and Jamie could meet at the Coral Gables Party Supply Store to choose the tables for Carmen's *quince*. Sharon Kim and her team were also there, filming all of the action. The only problem was that it wasn't quite as exciting—or natural—as the television team had hoped.

"I think you should do long rectangle tables forming a giant *U* around the runway; that way, everyone gets a great view of all the fashion coming out," Jamie said.

Carmen walked over to the high-topped tables. "I'm thinking that I should skip the formal sit-down altogether and just do stations of appetizers."

"People love stations," Alicia said, a little too brightly as she stared directly into the camera.

"Cut!" Mary cried. "Remember, girls, we're just flies on the wall. Talk to each other as if we weren't here."

"My bad, I'm so sorry," Alicia said.

"Roll 'em," Mary said.

"High-topped tables it is," said Carmen.

"Now, let's talk about linen," Jamie put in. "White or ecru?"

"Cut!" Mary yelled.

"What's wrong now?" Carmen asked.

"This is television," the producer said. "We need action, excitement. You're teenage girls planning the biggest party of your life. Can we *feel* the drama? Sharon, I think you need to jump in there."

Sharon, who had been standing off to the side, nodded. "You're the boss." She gave herself a quick pat of powder and ran a brush through her hair, then joined the *amigas*.

Mary arranged the girls around a table with Sharon in the middle. Out of nowhere, four Diet Cokes appeared, as well as glasses of ice.

"Ugh," Jamie said. "I never drink diet soda."

"They're our sponsors," Sharon said. "So, if you want a shot at the prize money, which they are providing, I suggest you pretend."

"I *love* Diet Coke," Jamie said, holding the can close to her cheek.

"No looking at the camera," Mary scolded. "Now,

this is just some good-old-girl talk. I want to hear about boys; I want to hear about dresses; I want to feel the excitement. Roll 'em! Again!"

The *amigas* tried not to notice all of the customers and store employees staring at them, and they did their best not to look at the camera. But it was a lot harder to just hang out with Sharon Kim, as if chilling with TV stars were what they did on the regular.

"So, Carmen," Sharon said, "tell me about your dress. Where did you get it?"

"I'm actually making my dress," Carmen said. "I make all of my clothes."

"Including the cute little number you have on right now?" Sharon asked.

"Yep," Carmen said.

"How wonderful!" Sharon said. "And what color is your dress going to be?"

"Well, it looks like this." Carmen took her sketchbook out of her purse. She flipped to a page filled with elaborate, colorful drawings.

"Are you getting this on camera?" Sharon said. "They are beautiful! I want to frame them!"

"Thanks," Carmen said, shyly. "The red, green, and gold represent the colors of the tropics to me, and this lion is the lion of Judah, which is a symbol of faith for many people and is for me a symbol of the strength I feel when I'm true to myself and to my culture."

"Now, you're Jewish and Latina, right?" Sharon hedged. "That's unusual."

"A little bit," Alicia chimed in. "But there are literally hundreds of thousands of Jewish people in Argentina, where Carmen's dad is from."

"Did you have a bat mitzvah?" Sharon asked, with a look that was hard to read. Was she interested for real—or for the show?

"No," Carmen said, shaking her head.

"How did your Jewish relatives feel about that?"

"Um, not so good," said Carmen, looking down.

"Did they feel *betrayed*?" Sharon asked.

Jamie put her arm around Carmen's shoulder and shot Sharon a warning glance. "That's kind of a strong word."

Sharon looked into the camera and said, "Caught between her Latin heritage and Jewish religion, a young bicultural girl struggles to find a place for herself in the melting pot that is Miami."

"Cut!" Mary cried out. "That was wonderful, Sharon. Good job, girls. So, where do we go next?"

"I've got Hebrew lessons," Carmen said.

"And I'm meeting Gaz to shop for silverware," Alicia added.

"I'm going to drive around to all the Goodwills and charity shops looking for beautiful old forks and spoons and knives that we can polish and put into vases on each table for people to help themselves," Jamie explained.

"Hmmm; what do you think will be most dramatic?" Mary asked Sharon, not addressing the girls.

"Hebrew lessons, definitely," Sharon said. "I'm really loving this whole Jewish Latina subculture. I think we could do a whole series on it over the holiday."

"I completely agree," Mary said. "It's got Emmy written all over it."

The girls exchanged glances and Jamie said, "Do you mind if we steal Carmen for a few minutes?"

"No problem," Mary said. "Just not too long. We're on a tight schedule."

The *amigas* stepped outside the store. "Are you okay with this?" Jamie asked, a look of concern on her face.

"It's kind of weird having them around *all* the time," Carmen said, shrugging. "They filmed my family having dinner last night, and they followed me from homeroom to history class the day before that. But it's also exciting. We've got to win this contest. *Quinces* are our business. We're *professionals.*"

"But they're also asking a lot of personal questions about your Jewish heritage," Alicia said. She lifted an imaginary microphone and, imitating Sharon, asked, "How do you feel representing the 'melting pot of Miami'?"

Carmen shrugged again. "There are worse things. I could be representing the cuckoos in Coconut Grove."

"Or the hoochies of Hialeah," Jamie said.

The girls started laughing.

"Speaking of Hialeah, have you heard anything about Simone and her mystery client?" Alicia asked.

"Not a thing," Jamie said.

"You know what?" Carmen said. "As much as I'd love to win this contest, what I really want is to have an amazing *quinceañera*, one that my friends and family won't soon forget."

"Don't worry. That's a given. This is going to be our best *quince* yet," Alicia promised, giving Carmen a hug.

"Because you deserve nothing but the best," Jamie said. She hugged Carmen, too.

"Cut!" Mary yelled, startling the girls. They had no idea they'd been followed.

"That was really sweet," Sharon said, turning to Mary.

"Yeah, it's those kind of tender friendship moments that will really make these shows work."

"You were filming us?" Carmen asked, surprised.

"You'd better believe it," Sharon said. "Between now and the finale, we're *always* going to be filming you."

That night, finally away from the cameras, Carmen began fitting her mother for the dress she was making her for the big day. Carmen's plan was to have all of the important people in her life strut down the runway in custom-made outfits.

"Do you like this fabric, *Mami*?" Carmen asked, taking out a bolt of emerald green material.

"It's beautiful," Sophia said.

"My idea is that your dress is really simple, but elegant, with an empire waist and a jeweled neckline, so the jewelry is sewn right into the collar."

"I love it, *niña*," Sophia said. "How lucky I am to have a daughter who designs couture clothing just for me. So, tell me, how are you feeling about this whole television competition?"

"Fine, so far," Carmen said. "But if we don't win the contest, we don't get to go to New York, and my friends will be so bummed."

"That's not your problem, *niña*," Sophia said. "Just like making *Abuela* Ruben happy is not your problem."

Her mother picked up Carmen's sketchbook and said, "All of your life, even before you learned how to sew, you've had this tremendous gift for being able to imagine something beautiful and then bringing it to life on the page. That's what your *quince* should be like. Your celebration should follow *your* dreams—not mine, not the TV people, not even your *abuela*'s. Because what you see and what you draw always comes straight from here."

She put her hand over Carmen's heart, then pulled her daughter in close for a big hug.

CHAPTER 10

CARMEN AND ALICIA were once again sitting in the boat, discussing boys and *quince* plans.

"I've seen Domingo every day since our date," Carmen said, taking a sip of her bottled water. "He's already agreed to be my *chambelán* at my *quince*. And while that is all well and good, my friend, I was wondering about you and Gaz. Have you talked to him about maybe going a little further than the flirtation?"

Alicia sighed. She looked back to shore. On the walkway, Carmen's Australian neighbors were dragging surfboards toward their house. She thought they'd beaten the early bird that day, but the surfers had been down to the beach, up on the waves, and were back home again—and it wasn't even nine yet.

"I'm going to see Gaz tonight," Alicia finally answered.

"Is it a date?" Carmen asked, intrigued. "You two

never go anywhere without me or Jamie to chaperone."

Alicia smiled. "It's not a date, it's a *thing.*"

"A thing?" Carmen asked, curious.

"Yeah. You know, a *thing,*" Alicia said. "I can't explain it. I mean, yes, we'll be alone, so it's a date but also just a thing."

"Can I offer you one piece of advice for whatever it is?" Carmen asked. When Alicia nodded, she said, "Just tell him how you feel. It's not like before, when there was all that uncertainty. Now you know he feels the same way."

"Hello, *chicas!*" Sharon called out from the water's edge, interrupting them.

"Not again," Alicia muttered. "Do they always have to be here right when we are in the middle of something?"

"Is it a day that ends with a *Y*?" Carmen whispered.

She and Alicia brought the boat back into shore and walked over to the TV crew.

"What's going on?" Carmen asked.

"It's time for the talent portion of the competition," Sharon said, in that perfectly upbeat television-news voice.

"Talent portion?" Alicia asked, sardonically. "Is this a beauty pageant? Or a *quinceañera*? Where's Raymunda?"

"She filmed her segment yesterday," Mary explained.

"What did she do?" Carmen asked.

The girls were becoming so used to the constant presence of the *Project Quince* team that they hardly noticed as Arnie miked them and began filming.

"Raymunda played the shamisen," Mary explained. "She plans to accompany her *damas* and *chambelanes* on it for their solo dance performance."

"And what, exactly, *is* a shamisen?" Carmen asked.

"It's a traditional Japanese instrument," Mary replied as though that were obvious.

"Look at this," Sharon said; it was Raymunda, on a portable DVD player.

"But she sounds terrible!" Alicia said.

Sharon nodded. "The thing that's so deep is that it's *supposed* to sound nonmusical."

"You see," Mary chimed in, "it's a song about the horrors of World War Two."

"And Raymunda says," Sharon continued, "that in Japan, when you want the listener to feel your pain, then you sing out of tune."

"Mission accomplished," Alicia sniped.

"So, what will your talent be, Carmen?" Sharon asked cheerfully.

"You know what my talent is," Carmen said, in a plaintive tone. "It's sewing. I'm designing and making all of the gowns for my family and my court."

Mary shook her head. "Not visual enough."

"Don't you have anything else?" Sharon asked.

"No," Carmen snapped. "There is nothing else."

"Your mom said you were wicked on the hula hoop," Mary said.

"Yeah, maybe when I was seven," Carmen said, fighting the urge to throw a temper tantrum worthy of a seven year old.

"Well, let's give it a whirl anyway," said Sharon, as she tossed Carmen a hula hoop that she'd apparently stashed behind a tree in Carmen's front yard.

Carmen shrugged her shoulders, then started hula-hooping, tentatively at first, then with more confidence.

"Looking good, looking good," Mary called out encouragingly.

Carmen continued to hula-hoop and was just beginning to have fun when Sharon yelled, "Try this one on your arm!" She tossed the girl a second hoop, and Carmen, who had been smiling, began to grimace and growl as she spun one hula hoop around her hips and a second on her arm.

"Keep it going; whoop, whoop! Whoop! Whoop!" Sharon cried out from the sidelines.

Three minutes later, Carmen let the hula hoops fall.

"Oh, too bad," Mary said.

"Are you kidding me?" Alicia asked in disbelief. "That's it?"

"Better luck next time!" Sharon said as the television crew prepared to leave.

When the two friends were alone again, Carmen began to cry.

"Don't sweat losing the talent competition," Alicia said, pulling her friend into a hug. "We're going to win this."

"It's not about winning," Carmen said. "It's just so embarrassing."

"Your hula-hooping was great," Alicia said, trying to be comforting.

Carmen shook her head. "I should have just walked away. All of this crazy competition stuff is just for show. It has nothing to do with my *quince* or about how to throw a banging party on a microbudget. This is just a . . . a . . . circus!"

Then, without another word, Carmen opened the front door and went into her house.

For their "thing," Alicia was meeting Gaz at the Florida Room, the old-school jazz club in the basement of the Delano Hotel. It was one of Alicia's new favorite spots.

She loved the cruise-ship curves of the walls and the giant art deco chandeliers that gave the room the perfect amber glow. She would have loved to have her *quince* in a place like the Florida Room. Too bad that at the time, a trip to Spain seemed like the most amazing thing to do. She'd learned a lot over the past few months about how important a *quince* was and the significance it held in developing one's identity as a Latina. She wouldn't admit it to anyone, but she sometimes wished she could do it over again.

She was taking in the architecture and imagining herself in a sleek art deco dress to match the interiors when Gaz walked in. His dark straight hair was just a little too long, though it looked good on him. He was wearing a tissue-thin black V-necked sweater, khaki pants, and black loafers—and Alicia thought that that looked good, too. He waved and made his way across the room.

Alicia had been at the club since it opened, at eight, so she had managed to snag an excellent table in the back. She thought she recognized a couple of people: a model who frequently appeared on the cover of *Ocean Side* magazine, a singer who allegedly kept an apartment—and girlfriend—in the Delano when he wasn't at his houses in New York or the Bahamas. But she couldn't be sure about either one. That was the thing about South Beach: everybody looked a little famous.

"Hey," Gaz said, sitting down. He picked up her hand and gave it a gentle squeeze.

"What's up?" Alicia said.

"Long day. I kind of can't wait until school starts up again next week. Working is for the birds."

A waiter came by and they ordered their usual virgin *mojitos*.

When the drinks arrived, Alicia looked at her watch. Eight thirty. It was summer, so her parents let her stay out a little later, but if she stayed out past ten, they weren't going to be happy about it. And her house was more than thirty minutes away, with all the traffic. She had to get right to the point.

"Look, Gaz," she began, "I don't know how to say it, so I'm just going to say it. I don't want a flirtationship anymore. I want to be boyfriend and girlfriend, for real."

The words came out quickly, and almost immediately she wished she could take them back. In the silence that followed, she looked around the club. She counted the number of people wearing sunglasses inside—four. She counted the number of girls wearing short shorts and heels—eleven. She counted the people with visible tattoos—seven. Gaz still hadn't spoken, and she wanted to look anywhere but at his face. Finally, when she just couldn't take it anymore, she looked at him.

"Did you hear me?" she said.

"I heard you," he said, staring down into his drink.

"Do you not want to be my boyfriend?" She could feel her voice shaking as the words came out, and then she could feel the tears just behind her eyes ready to tumble out, too.

"No," he replied. He still hadn't looked at her.

"Just no. No explanation?" she asked, tugging on her necklace. All of a sudden, it was as if she couldn't breathe.

"Nope," he said.

"That's really it?" Alicia said. She bit her lip and wished only that she could bite it hard enough to draw blood; in any case, she felt as if she were already bleeding.

"Yep," Gaz said. He finally looked at her, and his eyes were still dark and handsome, his lips were still plump and dark pink. He didn't look like a monster, but he sat there saying monstrous things.

"After all we've been through, Gaz!" Alicia whispered, to keep herself from screaming. "I'm going to ask you one more time. Do you have *anything* you want to say to me?"

Gaz shook his head and said, again, "Nope."

Alicia felt as if she were choking. Gasping for air, she ripped the necklace off and held it clutched in her fist.

"I'm out of here," she said, frantic to be far away.

Gaz looked at her again, and, for an instant, she thought she saw something tender, something not callous and cruel.

"What is it, Gaz?" she asked hopefully.

"Do you want a ride?" he asked.

"Are you serious," she said, trembling as she stood. "No, I don't want a ride—ever." Then she walked away.

"Alicia, wait," he said, getting up and running after her. "I want to explain, it's just that it's complicated, and I've been thinking about it so much, and it's way too important, and—"

"You're not making any sense right now," Alicia said, her sadness replaced with the beginning twinges of anger.

"I'm trying, Lici," Gaz said.

"Trying to let me down easy? Trying not to break my heart?" Alicia asked.

"All of that," Gaz said.

Alicia could barely hold back the tears. "Well don't bother Gaz. I'm a big girl. I can take care of myself."

She started to walk away and then stopped. "Oh, and

by the way, don't bother coming to Amigas meetings. You're not welcome." Then, with nothing else left to say, she turned and walked out of the club. As she made her way toward the taxi stand, she could hear the DJ playing "Tell Me Something Good." Good news would have been nice at this point—even just quasi-good news.

Even after she got home, brushed her teeth, changed into her pajamas, and got into bed, she still hoped she'd wake up the next day and discover that it had all been a horrible nightmare. But she knew that wasn't going to happen. Gaz hadn't said he loved her, hadn't told her he wanted to be with her. He had dumped her. And the worst part was, they hadn't even been going out.

CHAPTER 11

ALICIA LITERALLY didn't get out of bed the next day. Maribelle brought her some breakfast, which she didn't eat. At lunchtime, Maribelle brought her a bowl of gazpacho and a Jarritos soda. Alicia ate two spoonfuls of gazpacho and downed the soda.

Convinced that her Lici had developed a nasty summer cold, Maribelle then prepared a big bowl of homemade chicken soup for her dinner, which Alicia did not touch. After Alicia had fallen asleep, however, Maribelle did find several peanut M&M's wrappers underneath her bed, which gave her the reassurance that, while the girl might have been sick, she was not starving.

Sunday was spent the same way. Alicia slept. Watched TV. She did not return calls from Carmen or Jamie. When her parents offered to call the family doctor, she declined. On Sunday night, she took a shower.

On Monday, which was Labor Day, when Alicia still showed no intentions of ever leaving her bedroom again, her mother called Carmen and Jamie and told them she thought they should come over. School was starting the next day, and, clearly, Alicia's affliction was social, not physical. Mrs. Cruz called Gaz as well, but he didn't pick up, so she left a voice mail.

Carmen was the first to arrive, and as soon as she did, Alicia started crying. Once she had started, she couldn't stop. She had changed out of her own pajamas into a pair of ratty jean shorts and one of her dad's old Harvard T-shirts that she always wore when she needed comfort or luck. It seemed to her now that she was in dire need of both.

"I told him how I felt, and he blew me off," Alicia said, her words jumbled through the snot and tears. "He just kept saying, 'no,' 'nope,' 'no.' No explanation. No 'it's not you, it's me.' Nothing. Just mean. And cold."

Carmen had to admit she was surprised. "That just doesn't sound like Gaz."

"I know," Alicia said, embarking on a new wave of sobbing. She cried on Carmen's shoulder, then apologized for slobbering all over her dress.

"I have three little sisters," Carmen said, rubbing her

friend's back. "I'm not afraid of a little slobber."

Jamie walked in a short while later, dressed in a red and black plaid bubble dress over a pair of black capri pants.

"Is it about Gaz?" Jamie whispered to Carmen, who was still holding a sobbing Alicia.

"He broke it off," Carmen whispered back.

"What was he thinking?" Jamie asked.

Alicia sat up, her face red and blotchy. "You do know that I'm sad, not deaf."

Jamie sat down on the other side of Alicia and put her arms around her friend.

"Are you ready for some tough love?" Jamie asked.

Alicia shrugged.

"How long have you been in bed?" Jamie asked.

Carmen held up three fingers, as though Alicia couldn't see.

"You do know that I'm sad, not blind, right?" Alicia said.

"Three days is enough," Jamie said. "It sucks, but you're a strong *chica*. Moreover, you're a *busy chica*. School starts tomorrow. And Carmen's *quince* is only weeks away. That tropical synagogue is not going to build itself."

"What about Gaz playing at your *quince*?" Alicia

asked. "I told him he's out of the group."

"We'll get a DJ," Carmen said. "I love his music, but you're my priority. BFFs first, remember?"

The next day, Alicia was unaware of the back-to-school excitement. She pretended not to be looking for Gaz, but in reality she looked for him everywhere. Classes were a blur. A way to pass the time between "Gaz watch." By Friday, Alicia still hadn't seen him, and she was beginning to get freaked.

She met Carmen and Jamie in the cafeteria. Alicia was wearing a midnight blue silk jumper. She knew that only her friends had noticed she'd worn black or dark blue every day so far that week. But it made her feel good. She was in mourning. She sat down opposite her friends and slid her tray onto the table.

"What's that?" Carmen asked, pointing with her yogurt spoon to the pink and white scoop of something on Alicia's plate.

"Ceviche," Alicia replied.

"Raw fish, cooked in citrus, from the school lunch line?" Carmen asked, her face registering the grodiness factor at play. "Do you really think that's a good idea?"

Alicia pushed her tray away. What did it matter? She wasn't hungry anyway. "I think Gaz has changed schools. I haven't seen him once since we got back."

Carmen and Jamie exchanged quick glances, and Alicia caught it.

"What?" she asked. "What aren't you telling me?"

"We told him to keep his distance, or else," Jamie said.

"Or else what?" Alicia asked. The news that Gaz had been there all week long *and* that he had actually listened to her friends' threats was depressing.

"The 'or else' doesn't matter," Jamie said.

"What matters is that he did wrong, he knows it, and he's no longer welcome," Carmen said.

Alicia knew that there was nothing she could do. She hadn't dumped Gaz; it had been the other way around. How had it happened that the flirtationship, which was supposed to protect their friendship, ended up being the very downfall of it? Maybe it *was* her fault. Maybe Gaz had been the smart one, who knew that they could never have been more than friends who flirted.

"I cannot *wait* to go to New York," Simone announced, suddenly materializing next to their table. "That's right. When I win—and I mean *when*, not if—I think I'll use my prize money to go to New York and beat you at your Freestyle game."

Jamie glared up at the girl. "What are you? Some type of stalker?"

"No," said Simone. "It just gives me great pleasure to put little people in their place." She was wearing a gray off-the-shoulder top with a little sailboat print on the front. Her dark hair was ironed straight, and her lipstick was a deep burgundy color. It was a kind of preppy Goth look, and Alicia had to admit that Simone had managed to pull it off.

"Me, too," squealed Ellen, who was dressed to match Simone in a navy and white nautically inspired top.

Just what Alicia needed for lunch: dodgy ceviche and a hearty helping of haterade.

"The finale of *Project Quince* is coming up," Simone said. "Hope you *chicas* are ready."

"Yeah," Ellen said, giggling. "Ready to lose."

Her threat delivered, Simone marched off. Ellen, of course, fell into step behind her.

"I'm just so happy to be back in school," Alicia said, rolling her eyes. "Sophomore year. Best year yet. Not."

"We can't let Simone get to us," Jamie said. "Plus, our *quince* is way cooler than Raya-whatever. Speaking of, how are the Hebrew classes going, Carmen?"

"Good," Carmen said. "Normally, for a bat mitzvah,

you study for years. I just want to learn a few things to impress *Abuela* Ruben."

"That's cool," Alicia said, perking up a bit. "What have you got?"

They were all surprised when Carmen grew very serious and then, in a sweet voice, began chanting in Hebrew:

> *Oseh shalom bimromav*
> *Hu ya'aseh shalom aleinu*
> *V'al kol Yisrael*
> *v'imru amen.*

"Wow," Alicia whispered. "What was that?"

Carmen smiled. "It's a prayer for peace."

Only half joking, Alicia said, "Can you sing it again for me? I need some peace about the Gaz situation."

"And me," Jamie added. "Because there's a good chance that before *Project Quince* is over, I'm going to have to kick Simone's butt."

"What about Ellen?" Alicia asked, feeling in a light-hearted mood for the first time that week.

"Her, too," Jamie said.

Carmen began again, *"Oseh shalom bimromav . . ."* Then she stopped herself. "Wait a sec. Where did they say their *quince* went to school?"

"Hialeah," Alicia replied.

Carmen took out her phone and began typing.

"Who are you texting?" Alicia asked. "The *quince* police?"

Carmen smiled. "Nope. Even better. Domingo. He goes to Hialeah High. It's a big school, but a Brazilian Japanese girl named Raymunda is bound to stand out. We can get the scoop."

CHAPTER 12

STANDING AT Alicia's locker as dozens of other students swarmed by, it was easy to tell which three girls ran a full-time business in their spare time. Alicia, Carmen, and Jamie looked fierce.

There was no question, they *looked* great. But the expressions on their faces told the world exactly how they felt inside. That was impossible to hide. Jamie was afraid that if Amigas didn't win the *Project Quince* competition—and the prize money to get to New York—Carmen and Alicia wouldn't be able to come on the trip, and she'd have to attend the Freestyle Convention alone. It had been two years since she'd been back in New York, and she was a little nervous. She was a Miami girl now, and she desperately wanted her *chicas* to come with her.

Carmen was *exhausted*, and no amount of concealer could cover up the dark circles underneath her eyes. She'd settled on a color scheme for her Tropical

Synagogue fashion show—the Be Happy, Don't Worry Jamaican colors of red, green, and gold. But she had twelve dresses to create, not to mention the special dresses for her *abuela*, her mom, her sister, and Jamie and Alicia. She was also taking Hebrew lessons every day after school for an hour. Afterward, she ran home, sewed, stopped to eat dinner, and went back to her sewing. Una, who complained that the whirring of the machine kept her up, had temporarily taken to sleeping on an air mattress in the living room.

Carmen sewed every night until midnight, then got up at six and sewed for two more hours before school. And, oh, yeah, there was the little matter of the *quince* dress. She was supposed to be the star of the show, and yet she hadn't even started her dress yet. When she could, she claimed the TV and watched old episodes of *Project Runway* while she cut patterns. It was only the crazy schedule of that show that inspired her to keep going. Every morning, when she woke up, the thing she remembered from her dreams was Tim Gunn screaming at her, "Make it work! Make it work!"

Alicia, meanwhile, was keeping thoughts of Gaz at bay by pouring all of her energy and attention into the other details of Carmen's *quinceañera*.

You'd think that there would be nothing more fun

than to go shopping. But *quince* shopping is stressful, especially when you're in a rush and on a budget. Every day after school, there was a new assignment: tiara shopping, shoe shopping, makeup shopping, or jewelry shopping. And everything was either too expensive or not quite right.

And on top of that, everywhere the girls went, the TV film crew followed.

At school that day, free of the film crew for the first time in what felt like forever, the three girls walked outside to sit in the small garden near the front entrance. They were discussing another trip to yet another shoe store to try on shoes: flats for the pre-*quince* ceremony and heels for after. "You know what?" Carmen said. "Let me handle the shoes. What's next on our list?"

Alicia pulled out her clipboard. "Tiaras."

"Okay, Jamie, you're the queen of eBay; can't you find me a tiara online?"

"Sure, but don't you want to try it on first?" Jamie asked.

Carmen shook her head. "Nope, I trust you. Just remember, it should be less Princess in Taffeta and more Barefoot Contessa."

"Got it," Jamie said.

Alicia made a note of it. Then the three girls studied

the giant checklist that Alicia carried with her on a red Lucite clipboard everywhere she went:

- Make sure Jamie gets Carmen a vintage tiara from eBay. Budget is $30. Can go up to $50 if it's fierce. ✓
- Purchase delish red, yellow, and green cake with Jewish symbols on it. ✓
- Order custom bouquet for Carmen's quince: red dahlias, yellow gerberas, green lime leaves. No roses, 'cause Carmen hates roses. ✓
- Buy used circus tent from Craigslist. Must be cheap because Jamie's graffiti work means we can't rent one that we have to return. Must not smell like animals. Budget: $200. ✓
- Hire student photographer from school newspaper. Carmen wants her pictures to be black and white, photojournalism style. Make sure fotog takes color pics and video as well. Every quince changes their mind about their pictures at the last minute. Chances are Carmen is no exception. Cover our bases.
- Call the Hialeah Beauty School. Make appointments to look at portfolios of student

hair and makeup artists. Decide if any
of them are good enough to hire (doesn't
matter if they are working for free).

- Rent a red and green boat to dock outside
Carmen's house, so the boats match the colors
of her quince. (Fam. already has a yellow
boat.) ✓
- Take Carmen shoe-shopping.
- Choreograph dance for Carmen and Domingo.
- Find music for Carmen's vals with her papi.
- Find tango music for surprise dance with
Abuela Ruben and Carmen's papi.
- Pray, wish, hope that best friend has the
quince of her dreams.

Alicia stopped reading her checklist. There were at
least a dozen to-dos that weren't even on there, most of
them having to do with logistics of the set, decorations,
and music—all the stuff that Gaz usually handled.

"We need to nail all this down," Alicia said. "Can
you guys come with me to Bongos after school?"

"Bongos won't work," Carmen said, shaking her
head.

Jamie looked concerned. "Did something happen
with you and Domingo? Because it's too late to find you
another *chambelán*."

"No, we're fine," Carmen said. "We've just got to pick another place."

Alicia was confused. "Why?"

"Because my boyfriend shouldn't be waiting on us," Carmen said.

"I get it," Jamie said.

"I don't," Alicia said. "Someone else can wait on us."

"Spoken like a girl who's never waited tables in her life," Jamie clucked in a patronizing tone.

Alicia rolled her eyes. "*You've* never waited tables in *your* life."

"Doesn't matter," Jamie said. "I'm just saying, Domingo is Carmen's guy now, and therefore he's our friend. We shouldn't put him in a position where he feels like the hired help."

She bit her lip. "Okay, I get it now. Sorry, Carmen."

"Don't worry about it, *niña*," Carmen said.

"So, where should we go?" Alicia asked.

"Let's meet at my house," Jamie said. "I really want to show you guys how the graffiti work is coming."

"Perfect," Alicia said. "We can walk there, too. So, no need to try to get a taxi or a ride."

The girls gave each other high fives—exhausted, halfhearted high fives—but high fives all the same. As they made their way to their respective classes—

Carmen racing to her government class, Alicia heading to Spanish Poetry and Poetics, and Jamie running to honors chemistry—they all shared the same feeling: things were not quite okay yet, but they would be . . . eventually.

Jamie's house in Coral Gables was very different from Alicia's house with its pool, and Carmen's funky bungalow on the canals. The mint green home was a one-level structure, with a curved driveway and a small yard in the front. It had three small bedrooms, a large living room, and a traditional Florida room, which the family used as their TV room, at the back. Off the Florida room were a backyard and a garage, which Jamie used as her studio.

From the outside, the garage looked like any other: a door painted white with a small window cut into the front. Inside, it looked like an artist's loft in downtown New York City. Giant canvases hung from the back wall; Jamie had hung them gallery style, with invisible hooks and thin wires. Along the right side of the wall, shelves ran the length of the garage, and Jamie's custom sneakers were carefully lined up there. On the left, a parallel set of shelves had been installed, and these housed Jamie's many eBay purchases, each carefully tagged with the day it was bought, the amount Jamie had paid, and the estimated resale price.

"You know what?" Alicia said, looking around. "This is what the *Project Quince* crew should have been filming. It's awesome. You shouldn't even write an essay for your art-school applications. Just take a series of photographs of this place. Any college admissions officer will know that you are a serious artist."

"She's right," Carmen agreed. "I wish I had someplace like this for my sewing."

Jamie was pleased, if not a little embarrassed. "You guys are being too nice. But thanks. And C., feel free to use my studio any time you want. We don't have an Internet connection out here, so I have to do all my eBay hunting in the house. So I could totally be doing something else, if you needed privacy."

"Thanks," Carmen said. "I might take you up on that."

"You guys thirsty?" Jamie asked.

"Always," Alicia said.

Jamie opened the door to a little fridge plugged in under one of the cabinets. "I've got soda, I've got iced tea, and I've got water."

"Iced tea for me, please," Alicia said.

"The fridge is a nice touch," Carmen observed.

"It's left over from when my dad used to do his

woodwork out here," Jamie said, grabbing a bottle of water for herself. "He used to keep it stocked with cold beers."

"Where does your dad do his woodwork now?" Carmen asked.

Jamie grinned. "That's the thing. He had this set up as a workshop for ten years and only built one thing—that bench." She nodded at the piece of furniture holding up the fridge. "When my mom gave it to me as my studio last year, she said Dad could watch his games and drink beer in the Florida room like all the other fathers in the neighborhood! I've been fixing it up ever since."

Looking around the room, Alicia could feel her excitement for planning *quinces* and for planning Carmen's, in particular, coming back. There was no trace of Gaz here. "Show us what you've got," she said, determined.

Jamie took out a portfolio of drawings and *Tropical Synagogue*, the short-story collection that Alicia had given her for inspiration.

"The thing is that I think that excerpts from this book, while amazing, won't read so well in graffiti print on the tent," Jamie said. "Instead, I think we should choose iconic words to blow up and for me to tag the walls of the tent with."

"*Bashert* would be a good one. It means your 'fate' or 'destiny' in the Yiddish language," Carmen said. "I also really love the Hebrew word *aliyah*, which is what you call the trip to Israel. It means you always have a home."

"*Bashert. Aliyah.* I love it."

Carmen looked at the sketches. "You know what? This is an amazing idea."

"Yeah, whatever you think goes," Alicia added. "You've clearly got this."

Jamie grinned. "You mean, Ms. Cruz Control is going to let someone else take the lead?"

Alicia smiled. "Okay, guilty as charged. What can I say? The Type A thing is in my genes. Giving up control for me is, well, a process."

Jamie jumped up. "Okay, this is what I think we should do. The text should be classic New York subway, multicolored bubble lettering. There are dozens of fonts we could use, but I like 'Brooklyn Kid,' because it's easy to read. Check it out!"

She pulled a paper out of her journal and held up a printed sample in the typeface:

BASHERT

"I love it," Carmen said, clapping her hands together.

Jamie nodded. "So, I'll tag the tent with the words in this font, in Carmen's signature colors: red, green, and gold. I was thinking that instead of dotting the *i*'s, I'd write them as little palm trees, with the top of the tree replacing the usual dot."

Carmen gave Jamie a playful punch on the shoulder. "You do your thing, *chica*. They're not going to know what hit them at the Freestyle show."

Jamie shivered. "I can't even go there. Let's focus on giving you the best Lati-jew-na *quince* South Florida has ever seen."

Alicia was quiet for a second. "Lati-jew-na. That was Gaz's word." The smile on her face was replaced by a look of sadness. "How are we going to handle music without him?"

"You know what?" Jamie said. "Don't even worry about it. Now that my graffiti stuff is sorted, I'm officially on music duty."

"Okay," Alicia said, reluctantly. "Thanks."

"Hey, I wanted to show you guys one more thing," Jamie said before they could leave.

She pulled a large box out from underneath the worktable. "A while back, I got this deal on eBay. A hundred canvas bags for a hundred bucks. I always planned to tag 'em and flip 'em. But I was thinking that I could make them into gift bags for your *quince*, Carmen."

Alicia smacked herself on the forehead. "Gift bags! How could I forget gift bags? I suck. I'm the worse friend ever."

Carmen held Alicia's shoulders and said, "Deep breaths. It's not a one-woman show. Group effort, okay?"

Alicia sighed audibly. "Right, group effort."

Carmen turned to Jamie. "I love the idea of a gift bag that will really last. What are you thinking?"

Jamie pulled out another sketch. "I was thinking that I could tag these bags in a much more graphic style; something like this." She showed them an image of a subway car, covered in graphic bold images and colors.

Jamie continued, "Again, it would be in your *quince* colors. But the front of the bag would say, '*Hola*,' and the back of the bag would say, 'Shalom.'"

Alicia and Carmen stood in silence for a moment, and Jamie looked back and forth between them nervously.

"If you don't like it, we can do something different," she said.

"*Hola* and shalom," Carmen whispered, quietly.

"That's 'hello' in Hebrew, right?" Jamie said. "It's not offensive, or simplistic, right?"

"*Hola* and shalom," Alicia said, letting the words roll off her tongue.

"You hate it," Jamie said, dejectedly.

"I love it," Carmen said, staring at the picture of the subway-car graffiti.

"It's freakin' genius," Alicia added.

"I hate to be a spoilsport," Carmen said, "but do you really think you can tag a hundred bags in time?"

"Are you kidding?" Jamie said. "I live to tag. It's a done deal."

"Speaking of done deals," Carmen said, "I'd better run. My mom is taking me to the fabric store so I can get a few more things for my dress. *Hola* and shalom, *chicas*."

Then she gave Jamie a huge hug. "*Gracias, niña*. You did good."

Alicia hugged Jamie as well. "You did better than good; you did awesome. I'm really inspired."

Jamie shrugged. "Well, you guys inspire me."

Alicia said, "It's a mutual-admiration society."

"Exactly," said Carmen. "*Hola* and shalom, I'm outta here."

CHAPTER 13

ALICIA WAS SITTING at the lunch table waiting for her girls. She'd learned her lesson about the cafeteria ceviche and had brought in a Maribelle special from home instead. She was chowing down on the *cubano* sandwich when Carmen and Alicia arrived.

"*Hola, chicas,*" she said.

"Shalom, *niña,*" Carmen answered.

Jamie smiled and flashed them a peace sign.

"How's the sewing?" Alicia asked.

"Good," Carmen said. "Do you want to see some swatches?"

"*Claro,*" Alicia said.

Carmen reached into her bag and pulled out a bunch of fabric. "This green silk is for the bodice of the dress. Very simple: halter neck, natural bodice. Then I've got this gold silk that will drape all the way down," Carmen said.

"Where does the red come in?" Jamie asked.

"I've got this red silk that will be a color block at the very bottom, from my calves down to the floor," Carmen said.

"Not your traditional *quince* dress at all," Jamie said.

"Can you work some shalom into it, for your *abuela*?" Alicia asked.

"Already done." Carmen took out a bronze silk patch. "It's the lion of Judah. I'm embroidering a big one on my skirt and a little one over my chest, like the crocodile on a Lacoste shirt."

"Love it!" Jamie said.

Just then, Carmen's cell rang. Looking down she groaned. "It's a text from Sharon. They're outside."

At that moment there was a loud commotion as Sharon Kim and Arnie came rushing into the cafeteria. "I take that back. They're inside," Carmen said.

"It's *Project Quince* time, girls!" Sharon said cheerfully. "Meet us after school for an Inner Beauty/Outer Beauty competition at the mall."

"But I've got a ton of work to do on my dress," Carmen protested.

"You want that prize money, don't you?" Sharon asked. "Then *andale, niña!*"

"Raymunda and I will be there," Simone said,

appearing, as she so often did, out of nowhere.

"Great," Sharon said. She motioned for Arnie to point the camera at Carmen's sandwich. "Not afraid of a few carbs just weeks before your big day, huh?" Sharon asked, with an exaggerated wink. Then, turning to the camera, she said, "Teenage dieting epidemic. Story at eleven."

"But I'm not on a diet!" Carmen protested.

"Be at the mall at four, girls," Sharon said as she raced out of the cafeteria. "This is a competition. And every moment counts."

"That was *loca*," Carmen said when the crew was gone.

"You know what's *loca*?" Simone said, inserting herself into the conversation. "It's Gaz's score for our soon-to-be-award-winning *Memoirs of a Quince*. He's writing a song for Raymunda right now, as we speak. You know it wouldn't surprise me if he is so moved by her exotic beauty and the way she moves in her kimono that he totally falls in love with her."

Alicia's fists tightened. Carmen began to pat her shoulder, but Alicia shrugged her off.

"I hope they're very happy together," Alicia said, between clenched teeth.

"Oh, they will be," Simone said. "In fact, I believe

Raymunda may even invite Gaz to go with her to New York. Or are you so committed to losing that you aren't even thinking about the prize? I mean, really. Tropical Synagogue? *Puh-leez.*"

Simone turned and stomped away in her high heels. It was all Alicia could do not to throw food at her.

"Ignore her," Jamie said.

"I dunno," Carmen said. "Would Gaz really compose music for her? He knows what a snake she is."

"Well, she brings up a good question. How are *we* doing on the music front?" Alicia asked, trying to slow her racing heart.

"We're covered," Jamie said. "It's not live music. But my cousin, who deejays at Jay-Z's club in New York, Pulse, is going to send us a fully loaded iPod with everything we need for the *vals,* Carmen and Domingo's dance, salsa for the moms and pops, tango for *Abuela* Ruben, reggaeton for us. All we have to do is hit PLAY."

But Alicia shook her head. "That's not going to work. Amigas Incorporated never iPods the music at their parties. We bring a live band that's versatile and energetic. It's one of our signature offerings."

Jamie was taken aback. She knew it wasn't ideal, but she was doing her best to pitch in; couldn't Alicia see that?

"You know what?" Jamie said, the frustration and exhaustion of the past weeks boiling over. "Live music *used* to be one of our signature offerings. Then you started this stupid 'flirtationship' with Gaz, which was never a real thing anyway, and now it's over, and we've lost our supertalented live band and our set decorator and our transportation. . . ."

Carmen glared at her friend. "Quit it, Jamie."

Alicia stood up. "It's okay. She's right. I screwed everything up. Now I've got to be the one to fix it."

Alicia raced out of the cafeteria and then stood in the hallway, fighting back tears. She held her phone in her hand. She'd thought about texting Gaz a million times since she'd seen him last, but her pride wouldn't let her. Now she needed to put her pride aside and get him back doing music for Amigas Inc. It was what Jamie wanted. It was what Carmen wanted. And maybe, deep down, even if seeing him as just a friend proved to be a fresh slice of hell, it was what she wanted, too. After all, she'd been friends with him for a lot longer than she'd been crushing on him. She could make the friend thing work again.

She texted him: *We need to talk.*

He wrote back right away: *Where and when?*

She replied: *CG Plaza Starbucks. 6:15.*

He wrote back: *Fine.*

Not exactly a warm and fuzzy interchange, but at least he would come. That was all that mattered. Her stomach fluttered at the thought of seeing him, and her heart pounded when she thought of how cold he'd been. It was almost too much to take: the way all the sadness and fear and sweet anticipation swirled together. She took a deep breath, straightened the collar of her jacket, swept the hair out of her face, and tried to walk to her world history class as if she wasn't *this close* to completely and totally falling apart.

After school, the three girls went straight to the mall as Sharon had insisted. At the Gorgeous Gal makeup counter, they found Sharon, the camera crew, and Simone, but no Raymunda.

"Where's your *quinceañera* girl?" Jamie asked.

Simone shrugged. "I'm sitting in for her, because she's got a makeup exam she can't miss. Advanced physics."

"Sounds more like advanced bull—" Jamie began, snarkily.

Sharon wagged her finger. "Language! Ladies, please. This is a family show. So, this is your super *rápido* challenge: you've got thirty minutes to give three women Gorgeous Gal makeovers that are appropriate for attending a *quinceañera*, using the products here. In the end, you'll be judged not only on the looks you've created but on how pampered and well taken care of you make the women you choose feel."

Carmen shrugged. This would be easy. She'd been playing with makeup her whole life. And for special events, she always did makeup for her mom and her big sister. Alicia's mom, Marisol, had a natural elegance that her daughter had inherited. Both of them were so adept at applying makeup that no one ever knew whether they were wearing it or not. And Jamie? She was the hands-down expert in this category. She knew all the celebrities' cosmetics tips and secrets and for years had been brave enough to try out even the most outrageous looks.

Sharon went on. "Your judge is celebrity-makeup artist Carmindy."

The girls waved to Carmindy, whom they'd seen on countless reality shows.

"And your time starts . . ."—Sharon looked at her watch as if it were accurate down to the millisecond—"now!"

Carmen invited the first girl she saw, a teenager with a bad case of acne, to have a makeover. She gave her a clean, flawless face in five minutes flat.

"I love it!" said the girl. "I want to buy all of the products."

Carmen was finishing the girl's makeup when Simone came tearing back with an older woman with poor teeth and a smattering of facial hair.

"I've chosen this woman," Simone said, "because she represents our neglected elderly."

"*You're* neglecting the time," Sharon pointed out. "You've only got twenty-one minutes left."

By the time Simone had finished making up the elderly woman's face, Alicia had completed the makeup for their second "customer"—a twentysomething woman who worked on a cruise ship.

"The constant travel takes its toll on my skin," she told the cameras. "But Alicia made me, and my skin, feel pampered."

Sharon put the mike in front of the elderly woman's face just as Simone was finishing what was actually a very pretty makeover. "So, what do you think, ma'am?" Sharon asked, holding up the mirror.

"Not enough blush!" the woman said, reaching for a sample tube of lipstick and smearing it on her cheeks.

Jamie took the last customer, a new mom with a sleeping baby in a large stroller. Seconds later, Simone zoomed in. She too had picked a woman with a stroller.

Jamie was done first. Simone finished a bit later, right as time ran out.

"What's the verdict?" Sharon asked Carmindy.

"Well, clearly, Amigas Inc. has both speed and class. The women they made over felt good inside and out," Carmindy said. "I'd say there's no competition. Amigas Incorporated wins the day."

Sharon handed Carmen an envelope. "This is a gift certificate for two hundred dollars' worth of Gorgeous Gal products—and there's more. Carmindy will be doing your makeup on the big day."

The three friends all grinned. It had been worth it—completely and utterly worth it.

Simone threw down her makeup brush. "It's not fair! Raymunda's not even here. I'm just one part of our team."

Sharon put a hand on her hip. "That's your problem, not mine. Tell your client that it's absolutely imperative that if she wants you to win *Project Quince* she make it to our challenges!"

As Simone stormed off, Alicia gave her best friends a hug. For a little bit, she'd managed to forget she was meeting Gaz shortly. But then she remembered. This was going to be interesting.

• • •

Alicia got to the Starbucks at six on the dot. She felt as if she needed the home-court advantage of being settled in before Gaz arrived. She ordered a mocha Frappuccino and found a seat near the front.

Gaz came in only a few minutes later.

"Sounds good," he said, when she told him what she was drinking. "I'll go get the same thing and be right back."

As he went up to place his drink order, she tried not to focus on how cute he was and reminded herself that this was a business conversation. Amigas Inc. needed Gaz's band back. They didn't want him composing music for Raymunda. That was it. No need to get into anything personal.

Gaz returned, and, instead of sliding in next to Alicia, he sat across from her. Then, as if even that were too close, he inched his chair back and away from the table.

Alicia grimaced, forcing herself to concentrate. "How are you?" she asked, politely.

"Fine," he replied, in a monotone. "You?"

"Good," she said stiffly. "Look, Gaz, the girls and I, well, you, the thing is, we'd like you to still be a member of Amigas. We need you to do the music for Carmen's *quince*."

"I see," Gaz said.

Great, Alicia thought. Mr. Nonexpressive is back and in fine form.

"I mean, how could you agree to compose music for Simone's project?" she went on, her voice rising and her composure cracking. "Regardless of what happened or didn't happen between us. You know what she's like. I have to say I'm shocked you'd even associate with someone like her."

Gaz looked annoyed. "One, I am not 'associated' with her. At least, not yet. She handed me a *Memoirs of a Geisha* CD and asked me to listen to it. I said that I would. Two, I'm a musician. Just because I'm on the outs with Amigas Incorporated doesn't mean I'm going to stop writing songs and performing. You have no right to ask that of me."

They were nearly shouting now, and customers were turning to stare.

Alicia looked around uncomfortably. "Look, I'm sorry," she said, dropping her voice to a loud whisper. "We want you back. That's all."

Gaz also dropped his voice. "Okay, under one condition."

Alicia raised an eyebrow. "Name it."

"I want *you* back," Gaz said.

Alicia was sure that she hadn't heard him right.

"Excuse me?" she said. The words felt like boulders stuck in her throat.

He reached for her hand. "I've missed you."

She could feel the electricity when his fingers touched hers, but she pulled away all the same. She stood up. "Well, you should've thought of that earlier. You really hurt me, Gaz. We need and want you in as part of Amigas Incorporated. But I don't *need* or *want* to be involved with someone who could treat me so coldly."

Gaz looked confused, as though he had honestly expected her to come right around. "I said I'm sorry."

Alicia shook her head. "No. You said you *missed* me. Not the same thing, Gaz."

Then she stood up, turned, and walked toward the door. Turning back to him for a moment, she added, "Us aside, the others will expect you back. So, make sure you are at Carmen's for dinner on Sunday. And that you have her set list ready." Then, feeling slightly proud of how together she had stayed, she walked out.

CHAPTER 14

THE NEXT Sunday, all of Amigas Inc.—including Gaz—met at Carmen's house for dinner. *Abuela* Ruben had arrived and was making a pre-*quinceañera* feast.

"Where is everybody going to sit, *niña*?" Alicia whispered. "Your family alone is eight, nine with *Abuela* Ruben, eleven with your dad and his wife. You've got room for all of us?"

"Yeah, no problem," Carmen said. "My mom always says, once you're feeding eight, you're dealing in high-volume cooking, so the more the merrier. We're just going to lay out blankets and eat, picnic style, on the front lawn. By the way, Gaz is out front. I think you should go check on him."

Alicia rolled her eyes. But, it was her friend's house, so she headed outside.

"I really need to talk to you, Lici," Gaz said when he saw her.

Alicia looked unconvinced. "Can we do this another time?"

But Gaz took hold of her hands and gestured for her to sit down.

"Hear me out," he said.

"Fine. I'm listening," Alicia growled.

"High school romances are like milk," Gaz began.

"I know Carmen's studying Hebrew," Alicia said, "but that's no excuse for you to start talking in tongues."

"I mean, high school romances are like milk because they have very short expiration dates."

"Says who?"

"Says anybody with half a brain," Gaz replied, in a serious tone. "Couples break up. They go to different colleges, they break up. They go to the same college, become different people, and break up."

"So, what's your point, Gaz?" Alicia asked. He was clearly making an effort to express himself, but still, she was confused about what he was trying to say.

"We've got to stay in the friendship zone until we're old enough *not* to break up," Gaz asserted.

Alicia was incredulous. "And when would that be?"

"I figure when we're about twenty-five," he said. His voice sounded like the voice of a hopeful little boy.

"Gaz!" Alicia squealed. "That's, like, ten years from now."

"I can wait," Gaz said.

"But it doesn't even make sense," Alicia said. "Twenty-five-year-olds break up too." She could feel herself fighting back tears.

"I just want to protect *us,*" Gaz said. "I want to make this last."

Alicia sighed. For as long as she could remember, she and Carmen had been in the habit of renting DVDs and dreaming about the day when a boy would look at them like *this,* say things like *this.* Now that it was happening, she wished some big-time director would yell, "Cut!," so she could catch her breath and figure out the perfect thing to say and do.

"Gaz, there's nothing to protect if you hold me at arm's length," Alicia said. "I think if we both want it, we can make it last. But how can we if we don't hang out and you won't even kiss me?"

Gaz smiled playfully. "You still *want* me to kiss you?"

She nodded.

"If I kiss you, there's no going back to a flirtation-ship you know," Gaz said, leaning closer. "We could get hurt. Or break up . . ."

Alicia didn't trust herself to speak.

And then he wasn't talking anymore. He was kissing her. And it wasn't the short peck he'd given her before their "flirtationship" began. It was a serious, heavy-duty kiss that made it clear that they had just become much, *much* more than friends who flirted.

When she opened her eyes, she was surprised to see that her dream had sort of come true—just not in the way she imagined—Sharon and her camera crew had filmed the whole thing.

"Wait a second!" Alicia cried, reaching out to cover the camera lens with her hand.

"You're not supposed to be taping this!" Gaz cried, offended.

"You signed the press release," Sharon Kim said with a cheery, TV-anchorwoman smile. Then she turned to the camera and said, "The Catholic church has already denounced *quinceañeras* for being hotbeds of teenage passion."

"This has nothing to do with Carmen's *quince!*" Alicia cried, gesturing wildly behind Sharon.

"Forget it," Gaz said, reaching out for her hand. "They're going to show what they want to. We know what's real and what's created just for TV."

• • •

When Gaz and Alicia walked into the kitchen at Carmen's, the smells alone were nearly enough to fill them up.

"Oh, my," said Gaz. "What is going on in here?"

Abuela Ruben, all five feet of her, presided over the six-burner stove like a queen with a wooden spoon. Her hair was perfectly coiffed. The silk blouse she wore underneath her apron did not have a single wrinkle or stain. Her pencil skirt was conservative, but fashionable.

"Hello, Gaz; hello Alicia," she said in greeting. *"Dame besitos."*

Alicia and Gaz complied. Gaz put his arm around the older woman and asked, in Spanish, "What are you cooking that smells so amazing?"

Carmen's grandmother smiled. Older people always did when Gaz broke out his flawless Spanish. He was the only one of the group who was *completamente* fluent. And he used it to his advantage whenever he could, especially if food was involved.

"I'm just making a few little things," *Abuela* Ruben said modestly. "Chorizo Argentino and *salchicha parrillera*, grilled chicken, grilled steak, *papas fritas*—what you call french fries—with garlic and parsley, grilled corn on the cob, zucchini, fennel, and asparagus. It's a picnic, you know. So I'm keeping it simple."

Carmen hooked arms with Alicia and said, "The crazy thing is that she honestly thinks that's a simple meal. Come outside with me for a few."

The two girls walked into the herb garden and sat down on the two little wrought-iron chairs that stayed outside almost all year-round. They were painted white, with heart-shaped ironwork at the back. Carmen loved the chairs almost as much as she loved all the fresh smells—parsley, basil, radishes—in the garden.

"So, you and Gaz are good?" Carmen asked.

"Better than good," Alicia said, nodding. "Excellent."

"Yeah!" Carmen squealed. "I knew it would all work out, and when I saw your smile when the two of you walked in . . ." Her face grew serious. "But that's not why I dragged you out here. I asked Domingo about Raymunda. He's never heard of her. But he's got a cousin who works in the school office who's going to try to pull her records."

"Sneaky," Alicia said. "I like it."

"Carmen, your camera crew wants to come inside," *Abuela* Ruben called out in the singsong voice of someone who knew she was being recorded for television.

"I'm so sick of all this taping," Alicia said. "They snuck up on me and Gaz—midkiss!"

"Keep your eyes on the prize, darling. With cash money, we all get to go to New York with Jamie for Freestyle," Carmen said diplomatically as they walked back into the small house.

Sharon swooped in, blowing air-kisses at the girls. "Look, honey buns, we've already taped B-roll of Carmen's grandma doing the tango. It's sweet; it's going to edit into the piece nicely. Now all that's left is for you to really bring it at the ceremonies. That will be the moment of truth that will decide which team will be the winner. Thank you very much, to all of you. We're out of here."

Sharon sailed out of the room.

"What do you think? Do we even have a chance?" Carmen asked when she was gone.

"Well," Alicia said, "it's like what Barack Obama said in New Hampshire: 'while we breathe, we hope.'"

At the picnic dinner, Carmen and her *novio*, Domingo, shared a blanket with Alicia, Gaz, and *Abuela* Ruben. Jamie begged off dinner because she was on a roll spray-painting the gift bags, and wanted to get home.

As they balanced plates on their laps, Carmen said, "I really hope you like the way that I'm incorporating Jewish elements into my *quinceañera, mi abuela*. I never want you to be disappointed in me."

Abuela Ruben reached over and put a hand on her granddaughter's knee. "Was I disappointed that you didn't have a bat mitzvah? Yes," she said. "But that was in the past. I'm an old woman. I don't have time to hold grudges. I just thank God that He gave me the long life to dance at my granddaughter's *quinceañera*. You will have Latin music there?"

"Yes," Carmen answered. "Gaz's band is wonderful."

Abuela Ruben looked Gaz over with a haughty, slightly disparaging air. "And what kind of wonderful music do you play, young man?"

Gaz, who could hold his own with anyone, even a "snooty" *abuela*, said proudly, "Reggaeton, salsa, *cumbia*, merengue."

"What about tango?" *Abuela* Ruben asked. "*Somos argentinos.*"

"We're working up some tango tunes, too," Gaz said. "Don't you worry."

Abuela Ruben laughed. "Me, worry? Worry about yourself when I get you on the dance floor."

She got up and began to teach him how to do the tango. Sitting on the blanket, Alicia grinned broadly. This night was turning out to be pretty darned perfect.

• • •

The next day after school, Carmen visited her dad, who was filming a scene from his latest *telenovela*, when she saw Simone and her flunky, Ellen, who was wearing white makeup like a geisha's and a traditional Japanese outfit.

"Why is Ellen dressed up?" Carmen asked, moving closer to investigate.

Simone looked surprised to see Carmen. She tried to affect a calm look. "This isn't Ellen, it's Raymunda Itoi."

Carmen couldn't believe it! No wonder Domingo had never heard of a girl named Raymunda at Hialeah High. She didn't exist! Simone must have hired someone to play her (who then canceled), and now, somehow, Ellen was supposed to take over. Curious about how Simone was going to try to pull this stunt off, Carmen decided to play along.

"You remember me telling you about Raymunda," Simone continued. "She's Brazilian Japanese. From Hialeah."

"So nice to meet you," Carmen said.

Ellen just bowed. As. If. She. Were. A. Genuine. Geisha.

It was all Carmen could do to keep herself from screaming, *You've got to be kidding me!* She knew that Simone had guts, if not a whole lot of morals. She just hadn't known until now just how much in the way of guts and morals she really had.

"Since Raymunda's theme is Memoirs of a *Quince*, we're transforming the Biscayne Bay ballroom of my father's hotel into the red-light district of old Japan," Simone went on.

"That's pretty cool," Carmen told Simone insincerely. Then she turned to Ellen/Raymunda. "I gotta run. But it was nice meeting you, Raymunda. Have a great *quince*."

The minute she had gotten a safe distance down the hallway, Carmen texted the group: *S.O.S. Everyone meet at the Whip 'N' Dip. ASAP.*

Over bowls of fro yo, Carmen told Alicia, Gaz, and Jamie all about how Simone was putting together a fake *quinceañera* for a nonexistent girl.

"What do we do?" she asked when she had finished. "If we rat her out, she'll be disqualified and we won't win fair. If we don't, she could win. And Jamie won't get to show her sneakers at the Freestyle show in New York."

"This sucks," Alicia groaned. "I hate to be the one to say it, but Simone's got to be put in her place."

Jamie nodded. "Call the producer. We can't risk our New York trip on this crap."

Gaz shook his head. "No, let's not stoop to her level. Let's give Simone a chance to come clean. It's better if she confesses what she's done."

Reluctantly, everyone agreed. But one thing was certain: if Simone refused to speak up, they'd speak up for her.

After school the next day, Carmen and Alicia waited for Simone by her locker.

"What do you want?" Simone asked, walking up. She was very good at giving attitude, but Alicia could tell that her voice held just the faintest tremor of fear.

"Look, we know that Raymunda is really Ellen," Alicia said. "And we want to give you the chance to drop out of the competition before you get caught."

"Or what?" Simone asked, haughtily.

"Or we'll tell Sharon and Mary the truth," Carmen said.

Simone reached into her bag and took out a big manila envelope of receipts: for caterers, DJs, fabric stores, dry cleaners, party-supply shops. They were all receipts signed and paid by Amigas Inc. She waved them in the air.

"What's this?" Carmen asked, trying to grab the papers out of Simone's hand.

"Seems to me you spent well over the thousand-dollar limit, *chica*," Simone said.

Carmen was floored. "But these are all receipts from other *quinces* we planned."

"Not after I was done with my Wite-Out pen and my father's photocopier," Simone said. "One look at these and Sharon will have you disqualified from *Project Quince*."

"So that's how it's going to be?" Carmen asked, hardly able to believe that Simone would really resort to blackmail.

"Don't start none, won't be none," Simone chortled, a big, fat, smug smirk on her face.

CHAPTER 15

ON THE morning of Carmen's *quinceañera*, the *Project Quince* television crew arrived early at her house at 117 Millington Lane. They planned to capture Carmen's every move. Unfortunately, they didn't realize until 7:30 a.m., when the entire household woke up, how chaotic it would be to try to film a show in a small four-bedroom house with eight residents and twelve visiting guests, including a saucy grandmother from Argentina who let them know in no uncertain terms, "If you even point that camera in my direction when I have no makeup on and I am not dressed, *voy a matarte!*"

The twins, when not running between the crew's legs, made faces at the camera and jumped in Carmen's lap nonstop. Her brother, Tino, who was never far from his soccer ball, flubbed a pass that almost shattered an expensive light the crew had set up in the kitchen. Carmen's uncle Rogelio, who was slightly suspicious, refused to sign the press release until his lawyer had reviewed it—which he informed Sharon and her crew would take between forty-eight and seventy-two hours. At the same time, he would not vacate the kitchen, where Carmen's entire extended family was having breakfast, so the camera crew had to shoot around him, which was no easy feat, as he was six feet four and well over two hundred pounds.

"You know what?" Sharon Kim said to Carmen after about forty minutes. "We've got everything we need now. We'll see you at four, when the party starts!"

"Sounds good. And the deal is, you only stay at the party for the first hour," Carmen reminded Sharon. "I want everyone to be able to relax and have a good time, not feel self-conscious because the cameras are on them."

"That's what we agreed to," Sharon said. "We'll keep up our end of the deal."

Carmen was relieved to hear it, because she was still putting the finishing touches on her dress. She locked herself in her room, while the *familia* enjoyed a long brunch and the *amigas* set up the tent. She finished sewing at one. Her makeup was on by two. She was ready to go by three.

She kept poking her head out to look at the tent

where Gaz was arranging palm trees, Jamie was still tagging gift bags, and Alicia was walking around with her clipboard, looking stressed.

"Let me help," said Carmen, coming outside in a robe. She knew better than to put her dress on until the last possible second.

"Go back inside," Alicia insisted. "You're the *quince* today, not the hired help."

So Carmen went inside, where her mother had assembled a slide show of photos dating from the time Carmen was a baby until the present. Carmen groaned and went back out to the tent.

"Don't make me go in there," she begged. "My mom is showing *the* most embarrassing baby pictures."

"Well, you don't have to go back inside, but you can't stay here," said Alicia, who was now helping Michelle set up the food stations, including a table for the cake.

"Why don't you go for a boat ride?" Alicia suggested.

"Mind if I go with you?" someone said.

Carmen spun around. Domingo was there, and early. She wanted to pinch herself. He looked unbelievably hot in his tux.

"You're not supposed to see me until the *quince* starts!" she said, giggling nervously.

"I think that only applies to weddings," Domingo

said sweetly. "Let's go for a boat ride."

"In my robe?"

"I think that's best," he said. "I don't have a lot of experience with boats. I'd hate to have you fall in in your *quince* dress on my watch."

"Uh-huh," she said, nudging ahead of him. "It took over two hours to hook up my hair and makeup. I'll row."

"No problem," Domingo said.

At 3:45, Sharon Kim and her crew returned and began to film the guests as they arrived. It was a beautiful day—and scene, with the canal on one side and all of the houses on the left. At four o'clock, Alicia, who had changed into a simple red tank dress and a pair of Jamie's custom-made yellow and green sneakers, began to let guests into the tent.

There were audible oohs and aahs, as the guests walked around and read the words that Jamie had emblazoned, graffiti style, on the walls of the tent:

HOLA
SHALOM
A CELEBRATION OF JEWISH CULTURE
BASHERT

ALIYAH
FAITH

The potted palm trees that lined the perimeter of the tent, along with the high-topped bar tables covered in simple white linen, provided an elegant counterpoint to the words of graffiti:

IMMIGRANTS
MEANING
THE LION OF JUDAH
JOURNEY
SHABBAT
GAUCHOS JUDIOS

There were seventy-five guests in total, and the tent felt full, but not crowded. Capacity control was a huge thing with *quinceañeras* because both friends and family members tended to invite *their* friends to crash. It was always, "Yeah, come to my friend's/niece's/ cousin's *quince*. There'll be free food, cute girls/guys. It'll be *fun*."

"Nobody ever thinks about how much planning goes into a *quince*," Alicia muttered, "or how the head count, even with a buffet, is a very serious thing."

Gaz popped out of the tent. "Talking to yourself, *chica*?" He came over and kissed her on the cheek, as though it were the most natural thing in the world. Alicia was surprised at how much she liked it.

"Just going over all the details," she said.

"Well, stop worrying, and come to the backstage of the runway. Carmen's ready for you to do your part," Gaz said.

The *quinceañera* was to begin with a fashion show. But first, Carmen wanted to speak. The guests watched in admiration as she sashayed down the runway, which placed her smack-dab in the middle of the tent. She was resplendent in her red, green, and gold dress, and in a nod to her Mexican-Argentinean heritage, her hair was braided Oaxacan style, with gold, red, and green ribbons carefully stranded through. Her lips were ruby red, and her smile was as wide as the canal that faced the house. She held a stack of index cards in her hands, and those who looked closely could see that her hands were trembling even though her voice was strong.

"As most of you know, typically, *quinces* begin in a church," she said, reading from the cards into a microphone she held in her other hand. "There are traditional steps that you all know, so I won't go into detail. But I wanted a *quinceañera* that honored both my Latin culture and my Jewish religion, so I created this as a place where all of my roots could live. *Bienvenidos a mi* Tropical Synagogue.

"I wanted to point out that I am not wearing either the flats of the pre-*quince* or the heels of a girl who's gone through a church ceremony. I'm barefoot, with a rather cute pedicure, if I do say so myself, to symbolize my humility for the long roads my people—all of my people—have walked in this world and in this life.

"I wanted to tell you something about this dress. All of you who know me know that I have dreamed my whole life of being a fashion designer. My *abuela* Ruben taught me how to sew. When I was a little girl, I used to go down to Buenos Aires every summer, and she taught me a little more each time. First, how to hand-stitch without sticking myself, then how to use the machine, then how to make and cut patterns. I made all the dresses you'll see on the runway tonight. But I couldn't have done any of it if it hadn't been for her."

She paused to catch her breath and went on. "I have been studying Hebrew, and I want to read a poem by the contemporary Israeli poet Amir Or that symbolizes to me how you connect the past to the future."

Carmen read a stanza in Hebrew. Then she read the English translation.

> *This poem will be a poem of another century,*
> *not different from this one.*
> *This poem will be securely concealed*
> *under heaps of words, until,*
> *between the last sand grains of the hourglass,*
> *like a ship inside a bottle, it will be seen,*
> *this poem.*

She finished by saying, "There's one more thing. In a traditional *quince*, there are *damas* and there are *chambelanes*, because the girl whose *quince* it is is supposed to be like a princess in a court. But I wanted to change it up today, and instead of presenting a court to you, I wanted to introduce you to, and say a formal thank-you to, my Latina-Jewish tribe. All the girls are wearing Viva Carmen, and I do custom orders! Thank you very much!"

She jumped offstage, Gaz cued the music, and the show began.

Abuela Ruben was the first to go. She wore a red dress and a brocaded gold jacket and did a dramatic tango down the runway with her new dancing partner, Gaz. When she got to the end of the runway, she stopped.

In the wings, Carmen was puzzled. This wasn't part of the plan. The music grew softer as *Abuela* Ruben spoke. "Everybody knows me as the Jewish grandmother from Buenos Aires. I'm very proud of my granddaughter, Carmen, today, on her *quinceañera*. In Judaism, we have a tradition called the bat mitzvah. But *quinces* and bat mitzvahs share a common theme. This is when we welcome our girls into womanhood."

Abuela Ruben threw open her arms. "Carmen, where are you? *Ven acá, niña.*"

Carmen ran onstage and gave her *abuela* a huge hug. Gaz went back to the turntable, and Carmen and her grandmother held hands and did a tango move back down the runway.

Then Carmen and Domingo did a sexy salsa dance down the runway. When he reached the mike, the ultra-suave, ultrahandsome Domingo also surprised Carmen by saying, "Tonight is all about my girl, Carmen. She's got brains, she's got beauty, and she's got that Jewish Argentinean swagger. *Feliz cumpleaños, preciosa.*" He twirled Carmen around, leaning in to kiss her on the cheek.

Sharon and the camera crew came running forward. "Do the twirl again!" Sharon shouted breathlessly. "We didn't capture it on camera."

"Sorry, guys," Domingo said. "You've got to move like the paparazzi to catch a star on film."

Then he and Carmen danced back down the runway.

Carmen was in for more sweet blessings. Next up were Carmen's mom and stepdad. Sophia, dressed in a classic green shift with a rhinestone neckline, danced onto the runway with Christian to the tune of the Beatles' "All You Need Is Love." Microphone in hand, she said, "This celebration is such a reflection of my daughter, Carmen. She is a person who doesn't seek to define cultures, but lives it. *Feliz cumpleaños!*"

Javier and Natalia, who insisted on wearing her own hot pink Versace dress, came dancing out to the tune of Fergie's "Glamorous."

At the microphone, Javier said, "I produce *telenovelas* for a living, and that business is pure—"

"—Drama!" Natalia chimed in, throwing her arms up in the air in a diva pose.

"But this *quince* is above and beyond anything I could produce," Javier said. "To my daughter—and to Amigas Incorporated!"

Una, wearing a green and gold military jacket with a gold lion of Judah on the back, a gold cami, and a puffy black miniskirt, sashayed out to the tune of Shakira's "Hips Don't Lie."

"Everybody knows that Carmen is my little sister," she said, beginning her toast. "She follows in my footsteps in everything. Lately, she's been taking Jewish-studies classes, and I wanted to point to a certain lesson that is very important for all young women, especially a girl celebrating her *quince*. In the Jewish religion, women are believed to have a greater *binah*—meaning, 'deeper intelligence, intuition, and understanding' . . ."

The guys in the crowd began to call out playfully, "Boo!" and "No way."

Una shrugged. "I didn't write the Bible. Check it out: Genesis, chapter two, verse twenty-two. Women are built, not formed. I won't go so far as to say we're superior beings. But I will say that my sister Carmen has already shown great *binah*. Trust yourself, little sis, because you rock."

Carmen stood in front of the runway, her face covered in tears. It had been wonderful to watch all of her family strutting their stuff on the runway, to hear them welcome her into adulthood. But her sister's words sent her over the edge.

Domingo squeezed her hand. "You okay?" he whispered.

Carmen nodded. "I could use some air, though. Want to go for another ride?"

Domingo laughed, "What? In the middle of your *quince*?"

Carmen nodded. "We'll come right back."

They went out to the canal and got into the rowboat. Even though she was wearing a formal dress, Carmen steered the boat expertly along the calm water toward the footbridge.

"Your sister's speech really got to you, huh?" Domingo said.

"It's just been so crazy the past few weeks, trying to figure out how to do a *quince* with lots of Jewish flavor, wanting my *abuela* Ruben to be proud of me, having those crazy *Project Quince* cameras following me around. Then, when Una spoke, it was like all the dust cleared. When I was a kid and my *abuela* would come and make Passover dinner, there was a moment when the youngest kid in the room had to say, 'How is this night different from any other night?' Well, for five years, from the time when I was five until I was about ten, that was my line. So tonight, seeing Una, having you in my life, being here, with my family and my girls, I realized I've spent my whole childhood preparing for this moment. *Why is this night different than any other night?* Because this is the night when my grown-up life begins."

There was silence. Then Domingo waggled his eyebrows. "That's deep," he said.

Carmen stuck a paddle in the water and splashed him.

"Whoa! Watch the tux! I was being serious! Promise!" he cried, splashing her back, lightly.

"We should go back to the party," Carmen said, forgiving him.

"Is it okay if I kiss you first?" Domingo asked.

"What an excellent idea," she replied, leaning forward to meet Domingo's lips.

"I thought you would approve," he said, kissing her again and again.

It was a rollicking, casual, mixed-up *quince*—perfectly suited to Carmen's multiculti, laid-back style—and the *Project Quince* cameras captured everything.

But an hour into it on the dot, Carmen went over to the camera crew and said, "Okay, guys, you don't have to go home, but you do have to turn off the cameras."

Sharon smiled. "Excellent, because I really want to dance down that runway!"

And Arnie, who never spoke, said very quietly, "Do you think your grandmother would teach me to tango?"

Carmen laughed. "Absolutely! I'll introduce you."

After introducing Arnie to *Abuela* Ruben, Carmen unhooked her microphone and said to Alicia, "You know, we might not beat Simone's party. Fake *quince* or not."

Unhooking her own microphone, Alicia shrugged. "I know. But are you having a good time?"

"Are you kidding? Best night of my life. And you know what the best part is? There isn't a matzo piñata in sight."

"Then my friend, that's all that matters."

CHAPTER 16

THE FOLLOWING Monday, the members of Amigas Inc. were having lunch in the cafeteria when Simone came tearing over to them.

"You told!" she screamed at Carmen. "You told!"

"Told what?" Carmen asked.

"About Raymunda."

Alicia shook her head. "As a matter of fact, *loca*, we decided to take the high road, and we didn't say a word."

Just then, Alicia's cell phone rang and she excused herself from the lunch table as Simone stomped away. She returned with a huge grin on her face.

"We won," she said, in as calm a voice as she could manage. "*Project Quince*. Our segment airs this weekend, and we can have the prize money on Monday. Watch out, New York, here we come!"

For a moment, no one said a thing. Then Jamie jumped up and started dancing around. "I'm going to

Freestyle! I'm *go-o-o-o*-ing to Freestyle!"

Gaz raised one hand. "Hold up! You know we're going with you."

Jamie gave him a saucy look. "You guys aren't so bad."

"So who dropped a dime on Fakealicious?" Carmen asked.

"Well, when the TV producers went to Hialeah High to get some footage of Raymunda and couldn't find anyone who'd even heard of her, they got suspicious and began to dig deeper," Alicia explained.

"They *are* reporters," Jamie pointed out.

"So good triumphs over evil," Carmen stated.

"She's not really evil," Alicia said.

"Just deluded," Gaz put in.

"It's sad," Carmen remarked.

"*We* get to go to New York. It's great," Jamie chimed in.

"I meant sad in a great way," said Carmen, a wicked little grin lighting up her face. She had had a dream *quinceañera*. She had a dream boyfriend. And now she was going on a dream trip. No doubt about it, fifteen was starting off . . . well, dreamily.

CODA

A FEW WEEKS later, Carmen, Jamie, Alicia, and Gaz were all sitting on the airplane, bound for New York. Alicia's mom and dad, who had come along to chaperone, were up front, in business class.

"So, what's the first thing you're going to do when you get to New York City?" Carmen asked.

Gaz replied first. "I'm going to meet my A&R friend at the Bowery Ballroom. Check out some live music."

"I'm going to go to SoHo or up to Harlem or maybe over to Queens to check out the Chinese restaurants," Alicia said.

Jamie, who was relaxing behind a leopard-print sleep mask, lifted it to answer the question. "Freestyle. Javits Center," she said. "Why are you even asking me, when you know I need my beauty sleep?"

"What about you, Carmen?" Alicia asked.

"I think Jamie's got the right idea. As soon as we land, I'm going to the hotel to take a nap," Carmen said. "I love you all to pieces. But you wear a *chica* out."

A Chat With Jennifer Lopez

When I first came up with the idea for the Amigas *series, I thought about the many Latina women who, like Alicia, Jamie, and Carmen, had started out as entrepreneurial teenagers. Who, through hard work, imagination, and dedication, were able to take their passions and talents and become role models and successful adults. For me, Jennifer Lopez is such a woman. She has incredible drive and an amazing work ethic, qualities she shares with the girls in* Amigas. *They, too, needed an equal amount of determination to turn their* quince*-party-planning business into a huge success.*

So, to get a better sense of this connection, I sat down with Jennifer, and we talked about quinces *and what it was like for her to be a Latina girl growing up in New York City. Here are some more of her answers....*

—*J. Startz*

1. Carmen is determined to make all the gowns for her *quinceañera,* and her goal is to be a famous designer when she grows up. You're a designer with an extremely distinctive and successful clothing line. What advice would you have for her and other young designers who want to beak into this field?

Fashion is so much fun! I would advise Carmen and all young girls who have this passion to stay true to who they are. As designers, we are under pressure to deliver what's "hot," but I think if you really believe in a certain design, you should go for it!

2. The *amigas* rely on one another to solve their business problems, and each one of them has particular strengths. Whom do you go to for support and to ask advice when you need it? As a businesswoman and entrepreneur, what would you say are your strong points? What's really hard for you to do?

I surround myself with smart, trustworthy people from whom I get great advice. I feel that one of my strengths is my tenacity, a sense of never wanting to give up on things in which I really believe. I always remember that smart people surround themselves with smarter people.

3. Jamie, Carmen, and Alicia all are very tight with their mothers, and each of their moms has a very strong personality. How would you describe your relationship with your mother? Is she an important person in your life? Has she influenced you in your professional and personal life?

My mother and I are very close. She has always loved music and film and exposed me to it from an early age. I grew up listening to salsa music and watched a lot of musicals.

4. Jamie is the New York girl in the Amigas crew. She is also the trendsetter—in terms of fashion and picking up on the latest music. As someone who grew up in New York, do you relate to Jamie's innate sense of style? When you were a teenager, were you up on the latest styles? Looking back, were you ever guilty of any fashion disasters?

I love Jamie's sense of individuality! She's a risk taker, like me. When I was her age I definitely followed the trends but also liked to mix in my own flavor. I was a teenager in the eighties, so you can imagine some of the outfits I dressed in. We had so much fun getting dressed up I wouldn't swap a moment.

5. Carmen tries her hardest to come up with a party for her *quinceañera* that will make all of the members of her family happy. She has a big extended family, and satisfying them all is no easy task. Do you have a lot of family gatherings? Who is usually the party-planner in your family? Who's the peacekeeper?

We always had big family gatherings during the holidays when I was growing up. I loved being with my sisters and cousins—we have lots of girls in my family, like the amigas! *I would say I'm the party-planner of my family and also the peacekeeper. I just want everyone to relax, dance a little, and have a good time.*

6. The Amigas Inc. party-planning business relies on the group's ability to make their customers happy by throwing great parties for their clients' *quinceañeras*. What is the most memorable party that you've ever had? Did you organize it, or did someone else plan it for you? Why was it the best?

I have planned so many parties it's hard to pick just one! I do think that surprise parties may be one of my favorite types to plan. The look on the person's face when you yell, "Surprise!" makes all the hard work worth it.

7. Like the members of Amigas Inc., you're a very hardworking entrepreneur and businesswoman. What is your favorite way to relax?

I love to stay in, watch movies, and order a pizza. Oh, and having a luxurious facial and a massage isn't bad, either!

Make sure to RSVP for the next quinceañera!

Amigas
She's Got Game

by Veronica Chambers

Created by Jane Startz
Inspired by Jennifer Lopez

CHAPTER 1

ALICIA CRUZ, one of the founding members of Amigas Incorporated, giggled nervously as she boarded a boat moored to one of the more exclusive docks in Miami. Following close behind were her two best friends, Carmen Ramirez-Ruben and Jamie Sosa. They quickly mimicked her unusually high-pitched laugh. Shooting them a disapproving look, Alicia tried to regain her composure. After all, this wasn't just an ordinary hanging-out-with-her-friends kind of Saturday; they had a business to run.

The previous summer, Alicia, Carmen, Jamie, and Alicia's boyfriend, Gaz, had started a business planning *quinceañeras*, or Sweet Fifteen parties. And even though the friends were only teenagers themselves, they'd quickly become the hottest game in town.

They knew how to make a celebration that was modern but respectful of tradition; innovative; and, most importantly, not corny. A *quince* was like a wedding, debutante ball, and graduation all rolled into one, and Amigas Inc. had perfected the art of making their *quinces* rock. Still, no matter how many they planned, there were bound to be surprises. And certainly, when they had woken up that morning, none of them had imagined that they'd be taking a private ferry to the Mortimer family estate.

Growing up in Miami pretty much provided assurance that by the time you reached high school you'd have been on or around every type of boat, pontoon, and Jet Ski there was. What made the Mortimers' boat, the *Santa Maria* (the name was scrawled across the side), different was that literally everything on it smelled of money, from the polished oak floors to the shiny brass flagpole to the gold-stitched, monogrammed life jackets. Coral Gables had its share of rich kids, including Alicia Cruz. But Binky Mortimer and her golf-champ brother, Dash, were on a whole other level. And everything about the family ferry, which in any other part of the world would have been called a yacht, confirmed the fact that this was not the kind of wealth you encountered every day. Nor, Alicia suspected, was their destination the kind you encountered every day.

Miami was surrounded by dozens of small islands.

The most famous of these was Fisher Island where Oprah Winfrey had a house. But even Oprah lived on an island with other people. The Mortimers, as far as the girls knew, were the only family in Miami to live on their *own* island.

Considering all that (from living in Miami and reading the daily gossip blogs), it was not a stretch to say that Alicia had been surprised—no, make that floored—when she received an e-mail from *the* Binky Mortimer early in the morning saying that she wanted to hire the Amigas for her *quinceañera*. It had read:

Yo-delay-lihoo. I'm having a *quince*, and it's going to be hotter than the three-pepper special at Taco Bell. I hear Amigas Inc. is the only gig in town that can pull this throwdown off. So, as Donald Trump would say, "You're hired." Come to my island at 3 p.m. for a meeting. XO, XO, Binky.

Alicia knew that saying no was out of the question. She had quickly told the rest of the group and asked if they were up for a meeting after school. Their reactions had varied. Carmen had flipped at the idea. Jamie had rolled her eyes and said something about "another snobby sitch in the making." And Gaz? Well, he had just asked, "Who?" Apparently, he did not read the Miami social pages, and perhaps, Alicia had joked, he lived under a rock.

Now, standing on the deck of the Mortimers' private ferry, the conversation returned to the most popular topic since they had agreed to meet Binky. Alicia and her girls were of decidedly different minds about whether a non-Latin girl could or *should* have a *quince*. Carmen, who'd just thrown a "Hola, Shalom!" *quince* that celebrated her Latin heritage and Jewish religion, was all for it.

"Being Latin is all about being inclusive," Carmen said. "Our people represent practically every skin color and dozens of nationalities. We're a *global* culture."

Carmen was nearly six feet tall and had flawless *café con leche*–colored skin. Her dark hair fell in waves down her shoulders. She looked like a model, but designing clothes was her passion. She was dressed for the Mortimer meeting in a Carmen original, a hot pink one-shouldered blouse with a pair of wide-legged khaki pants.

Alicia nodded in agreement. But her mind was more on the money than on the culture. "Do you know how much money we could make planning a Mortimer party? Money is no object for Binky Mortimer, people. This will take Amigas Incorporated to the next level."

Her eyes sparkled as the headlines and gossip-blog

postings flashed through her mind. Alicia's drive for success was hereditary. She was the daughter of Marisol and Enrique Cruz, who made up one of Miami's power couples. Her mom was a judge, and her dad was the deputy mayor. Alicia had an engaging smile, cascading mahogany curls, and a flair for vintage style, aided by the fact that her mom had one of those huge walk-in closets like Carrie Bradshaw's in *Sex and the City*. Today she was dressed in an original DVF leopard-print wrap dress and a pair of Forever 21 pumps. Her goal? To look like the head *chica* in charge.

Though Carmen and Alicia had been pals since elementary school, Jamie had only joined the posse in junior high. Her skin was naturally bronze, with a tan that was the envy of South Beach, and she had dark, stick-straight hair. Jamie had the graceful build of a dancer and the "don't-mess-with-me" attitude of a prizefighter. It was an unusual combination, but on Jamie, it worked. She was from the Bronx, and while her attempts to "keep it real" could sometimes be a real pain in the butt, Jamie, as Alicia and Carmen knew, succeeded at them. She was the third Musketeer. Without her, they would just have been your run-of-the-mill "besties."

The sole male member of Amigas Inc. was Gaz (short for Gaspar) Colón. Gaz was a promising musician and an all-around great guy. Gaz's father had died when he was young. To help supplement the modest income his mother made as a cleaning woman, Gaz worked part-time, after school and on weekends, as a salesman at the Gap. This added responsibility made the amount of time he could spend with Amigas Inc. somewhat limited. But he did what he could.

He and Alicia had met in the sixth grade, when Alicia had enlisted him to play in her newly formed ska band. The band was short-lived, but their friendship was not. After many years of being buddies, followed by a brief "flirtationship," they finally admitted that their feelings had blossomed into something greater, more akin to love. Now they were officially together, and Alicia felt a familiar fluttery feeling as she thought about him. She just wished he could be there now, and not at the Gap, so that he could experience all of this with her and the rest of the group.

Suddenly a crew member in a crisp white shirt and black bow tie approached, cutting into Alicia's thoughts and interrupting the *quince*-or-not-to-*quince* debate. In a faint British accent, he offered them "a refreshment," and held up a silver tray with three sodas, three glasses of ice, a dish of lemon wedges, and a small silver bowl of bananas.

"Wow, thanks," Alicia said, taking the glass that was handed to her and resisting the urge to call the man Jeeves.

"This is nuts," Carmen whispered. "It's a fifteen-minute boat ride and they offer snacks." Jamie either was unimpressed or didn't care about the serious fabulosity of their boat ride. She had resumed her monologue outlining her issues with the idea of Binky's *quince*. "You let white guys rap and you end up with more Vanilla Ices than Eminems. You let *gringas* have *quinces* and next thing you know, Miley Cyrus will be recording in Spanish and winning all the Latin Grammys. *Unas cosas deben ser solo nuestras.* Some things should be just for us."

Alicia and Carmen stifled giggles. They had been hearing this nonstop since they'd made their decision to meet with the client. But they were now on the boat, and nothing could be done to avoid the meeting. "Let's hold off on the judging till we actually meet Binky, 'kay, Jamie?" Alicia said, a teasing tone in her voice.

Jamie shrugged. "Fine, whatever. I'm just saying."

"We know, we know. Just for us. Got it," Carmen said, laughing.

The waves parted as the ferry slowed on its approach to the Mortimers' home. The girls stopped debating for a moment to take in the turquoise blue waters, the lush green landscape of palm trees that shimmered before them, and . . . the two cute boys in kayaks who paddled past them.

"*Hola*, beautiful ladies!" one guy called out, causing the girls to blush. His T-shirt said UNIVERSITY OF MIAMI. Even though Carmen and Alicia had boyfriends, they both smiled and waved.

"Which one of you lovely ladies is single?" the second boy in the kayak called out. He had curly blond hair and he, too, was wearing a U. of Miami T-shirt.

"She is!" Alicia and Carmen called out in unison, pointing to Jamie and cracking up.

"What's your phone number, single girl?" the boy called out. "I've got a photographic memory."

"It doesn't take a photographic memory to memorize a seven-digit number," Jamie called back. "You're not smart enough to date me."

The boy looked wounded and mimed being shot in the heart. His friend said something they couldn't hear, and then the boys paddled away.

"He was cute," Carmen said, as the girls flopped down on the comfortable seats that lined the deck. "You should have given him your number. . . ."

To be continued . . .